THE WOLF IN THE GARDEN

ALFRED H. BILL

CENTAUR PRESS
Distributed by
COMO SALES, INC.
799 Broadway   New York 10003

First published in 1931.

Centaur Press edition, February 1972
Printed in the United States of America
SBN 0-87818-008-7

Distributed by:
Como Sales, Inc., 799 Broadway
New York, New York 10003

Cover:
Adapted from a drawing by Virgil Finlay
from the book VIRGIL FINLAY
(Donald M. Grant, Publisher,
West Kingston, Rhode Island 02892 - 1971).
Printed by permission of Beverly C. Finlay.

Centaur Press Colophon:
    Lawan Chomchalow

I. – ON GALLOWS HILL

"Robert," said my Uncle Barclay, "step to the door and see if the packet has been signalled."

I slipped down from my high stool reluctantly. It was a treat for me to be called in from the counting-room to work on my uncle's private ledger when the rector and Squire Killian happened to have dropped in. A discussion that began with politics, and might end anywhere, was sure to get going between those two, and the violent breaking off of my studies was still recent enough to make me welcome such a diversion from the monotony of commerce and account. When I returned, the air about them was gray with the films of their tobacco smoke, their chairs were drawn up to the glow of the Franklin stove – for the chill of the autumn morning still lingered in the snug, low room – and they were hard at it. Evidently it was the rector's particular hobby, the study of witchcraft and kindred superstitions, that had drawn the lawyer's fire.

"But, my dear Sackville," he protested, his voice shrill with irritation, his lean arm thrust forward as if he meant to impale the clergyman with the slender pipe-stem held in prolongation of it, "you talk as if you believed in all this discredited hocus-pocus."

"I read on good authority that King Saul visited the Witch of En-dor," Mr. Sackville replied calmly. "And in the same volume there is the divine command, 'Ye shall not suffer a witch to live.' "

"In the Bible, thousands of years ago, yes. But you talk as if you might believe that the wretched old woman whom they hanged up here at the top of the town a hundred and twenty years ago might actually have been a witch."

"Because an innocent man is hanged for murder now and then you don't ask me to believe that there are no real murderers, do you?" the rector parried.

"Of course not. But we have murder committed, proved and established, every few days."

"The same could be said of witchcraft up to a little more than a century ago."

"A century ago, yes. But what has become of it – of its practitioners?"

"My dear Killian," Mr. Sackville retorted, "if murder were a difficult art, only to be acquired by years of laborious study, and if all power of Church and State had been concentrated upon its extirpation for five hundred years, if every book on the subject and every person suspected of knowledge of it had been burned with fire, what evidence of its existence should we have in the world today?"

3

The lawyer's thin cheeks were puffed with his impatience to reply, but he changed his mind and laughed instead.

"Much learning doth make him mad, eh, Barclay?" he appealed to my uncle, whose natural indifference to any discussion which he regarded as useless was heightened by his eagerness for a report from me as to the arrival of the packet-sloop from New York. "How dare you talk such nonsense before your Senior Warden, Dominie?"

"So long as he keeps it out of his sermons . . . " My uncle's great laugh sounded even more perfunctory than usual, it ended so abruptly. "What of the packet, Robert?"

"Signalled, sir, ten minutes ago."

"Then have the goodness to go down to the landing. You may put yourself at Monsieur de Saint Loup's disposal for the rest of the day, should he desire it. I gather that he is not ignorant of our tongue, but he might be glad to have someone who speaks French at his elbow."

Because I had spent a month in Paris before my father's death and the ruin of his fortune had recalled me from my travels to seize with gratitude the place which my uncle had made for me in his counting-house, Uncle Barclay persisted in believing that I had a fluent command of French. For my part I wondered what I would do if this stranger turned out to be another of those haughty, inept aristocrats of whom we had seen only too many since the fall of the Bastille and the subsequent disorders had made their own country unsafe for them. I was somewhat reassured, however, by the thought of the letter introducing Monsieur the ci-devant Comte de Saint Loup which had come from my uncle's bankers in New York the week before. They wrote of him not only as a person of excellent credit but also as a cultivated gentleman who would be an addition to the social life of any community. He had some idea, they added, of making his home in some such retired town as ours until conditions should favor his return to France. And two minutes after meeting him, his fluent and voluble English and easy manner had dispelled my fears entirely.

At first sight — God save the mark! — he struck me as disappointingly commonplace: there was such a comfortable rotundity about his middling stature; dark as a Spaniard though he was, such a glow of health and good-living mantled his cheeks; and his forehead was so singularly unlined for a man who appeared to be close to forty years of age. Under eyebrows whose fine arches seemed never to have been contorted by a frown the peculiar tawny lights in his small black eyes sparkled as with a restless search for fun. His red lips were forever curving in a smile. All that he saw in our little

4

up-river town, which was already beginning to be forgotten and left upon one side in the rush of the new commerce up to Albany and into the opening west, appeared to excite his pleasure and drew forth his lively comment. He spoke in a voice surprisingly strong and deep for so small and merry a man. But each remark was prefaced by a chuckle like a sort of jolly growl, and his white teeth would flash back to the long, clean canines.

When I had showed him his lodgings, he suggested that I should act as his guide for a walk about the place. I began to say that there was nothing to be seen of particular interest for such a man as he, that I had been to Paris and knew what European towns, even small ones, had to offer to the sightseer. But he stopped me with his deep chuckle and a white plump hand raised in protest. He was a countryman, I must understand, living in the rural depths of the province of Auvergne, hardly better than a peasant and caring as little for the sights of towns as he did for Paris. It would be a dull countryside, moreover, that could seem uninteresting on such a glorious day, and if I must have a better reason for absenting myself from my duties he implored my services on a sort of preliminary tour of househunting. For of all the places he had seen in America this struck him most favorably as the spot whereon to plant his vine and fig tree.

It was indeed a day of the best October sort: the sun strong but temperate, the warm breeze spiced with the scent of the bending orchards and laden vineyards that clothed the slopes of the nearer hills. White sails gleamed on the flashing river; the tiles on the few old Dutch houses spared by the great fire of 1785 glittered against the autumnal splendor of a plantation of maples; and far away the fantastic outline of the Catskills glimmered through the blue haze. As we went along I pointed out the new beacon at the end of the old mole, the mounded trace of what had been the fort of the earliest settler, the rope-walk, the tannery and the sawmill, and Saint Michael's church whence, seventeen years before, Mr. Sackville had been dragged at the end of a halter by enthusiastic patriots because, good American though he was, he had persisted in praying for King George as his ordination vows required.

And while I was showing the town to Monsieur de Saint Loup, I was of course showing him to the town. People peered from their windows, shopkeepers made errands to their doors, to watch us pass. For in those small, steep streets where every man's face and most of his business were known to each other, this stranger in his black clothes of foreign cut, his immaculate ruffles and powdered hair, his silver-buckled shoes and plain walking sword of black and silver, would have been remarked

5

even without the air of distinction which he undoubtedly bore about him in spite of his ready affability. For the interest which he excited evoked his amusement like everything else. He nodded and smiled at the starers, waved a hand in jovial salute if one bowed in response, and more than once gave that deep growling chuckle when his advances were met with yokel-like stolidity.

Soon after we had turned up-hill out of the High Street he stooped with soft hand extended to speak to a dirty little urchin of a girl who, backed against a hoarding, her crooked mouth agape, devoured him with pale, lack-luster eyes from beneath an unkempt shock of straw-colored hair. Had I been alert, I would have warned him, for she was Jan Van Zile, the town drunkard's child, Aggie, whose malignant, half-witted mischievousness was a scandal to the community. Suddenly she spat at him, clawed at his hand with filthy finger nails and fled with a kind of choking scream, while the great mongrel cur which was her constant companion crouched snarling as if about to spring at his throat. I cannot describe the sound he made at that. I thought for a moment that he chuckled again. But there was no mirth now in that deep note. His face, when I looked at him, had gone dark crimson; his eyes glowed, reddish where the tawny lights had been. The cur cowered in his tracks, shivering, until we had passed on.

"An old countryman's trick with us," he explained airily, swinging his light cane by its silken tassel, in reply to the look of wonder and curiosity which I fear that I fixed upon him with more earnestness than was altogether polite. "Nothing more. All dogs detest me — except my own."

"You have a dog?" I asked, surprised, for I had seen his trunk and portmanteau.

"In New York — I left him with my heavier luggage — a splendid creature. I shall write for him to be sent me as soon as I can find a place to call my own. Now that," he broke off, halting before the rusty iron gate of a small, low house just visible behind the dead overgrowth of a garden that lost itself in a wildnerness of pine and hemlock trees at the back, "that is a place exactly to my mind, secluded yet accessible, predominating yet inconspicuous. I must have that."

We had been climbing the steep way, half street, half road, that leads up into the fields and woodland of the nearer hilltops and had left the town itself below and a short half mile behind us. The house before which he had paused was the last of a straggling fringe. Old Peter Armitage, the miser, lived there. So I told Monsieur de Saint Loup that he would probably have to wait for some time to obtain possession of it, since the old man seemed to be as tenacious of life as of

6

everything else.

"A miser, you say?" he asked sharply, and added after that amused growl of his, "but that simplifies everything. I am quite accustomed to paying for my fancy when I find it."

I explained that a rich man from New York had lately taken a liking to the place for his country residence, but that old Peter had refused every inducement to sell. It had been pretty generally whispered about that the old man could never have dug up and moved secretly all the money he had buried there, I added, and that his inability to do so accounted for his refusal of a very handsome offer.

"I shall have it nevertheless," my companion insisted. "He shall not refuse me."

There seemed to be nothing to be said in response to such stupid obstinacy as that, so I changed the subject.

"Yonder, sir, is the last of our local curiosities, I believe, Gallows Hill." I pointed to a small conical eminence a couple of hundred yards to our front, beneath whose naked summit the road wound its gray streak of dust between fields black from the fall plowing. At once he was his amused and interested self again.

"So even here, in this land of liberty and plenty," he moralized smiling, "man must have the shadow of death upon him to keep him from evil-doing."

Well, this had been quite a special gallows, I told him. Only one person had ever been executed upon it, and that a notable in her poor way — the only witch ever put to death within the borders of the colony, at least after the English occupation.

"A witch executed here, in this land of enlightenment!"

I had to smile at his tone of horrified amazement.

"More than a hundred years ago," I explained.

"Ah! Surely none could be found here to take such things seriously today."

"Seriously? No. Not in the sense you mean, if we except a few of the Dutchmen on the remoter farms, perhaps. The Reverend Mr. Sackville, the rector of Saint Michael's, of whom I told you as we were passing the church, has made some study of witchcraft to amuse his leisure."

"A minister of religion dabbling in the Black Art? You astonish me."

I looked at him twice to make sure that he was not playing with me, so profound was the note of reprehension in his voice. The rector's interest was purely historical, I assured him, but I understood that the rector believed God had in times past accorded to the Devil and those who became his servants power in the world, which mankind with the Divine assistance had gradually frustrated.

7

"He holds that this process of frustration is now complete?"

"It pleases him sometimes to maintain the thesis that we have no evidence of its entire completion," I replied, thinking of the debate which I had left in my uncle's private room and what I knew from past experience would be the next position into which Mr. Sackville would be driven by the lawyer's arguments. But Monsieur de Saint Loup appeared to have lost interest in the subject before I had finished speaking.

"Let us look at the house again. It suits me perfectly."

We had already lingered about the place too long to please its eccentric owner, however. I caught a glimpse of a familiar, threadbare green coat above the wall; and the bony head and calloped neck of old Peter writhed out between a clump of dead hollyhocks and the dried-up clusters of giant larkspur which made an almost impenetrable labyrinth of the garden paths, peering at us with purblind eyes.

"Be off with ye! What business have ye to block the road before my house?" he cried in a voice that cracked with the impotent fury of age.

"It is only Robert Farrier, Mr. Armitage," I shouted. For although generally he was regarded with hatred and contempt which he returned with interest, I had what by comparison might be called a sort of friendship with him. As a small boy I had gone to his assistance one winter's day when he had slipped on an icy sidewalk and broken his arm, and he had never failed to acknowledge the memory of this small service by a surly nod.

"I am showing a French gentleman about the town," I added, "and he stopped to admire your house and garden." But it was in vain that I thus tried to stretch his liking of me to cover my companion.

"Tell the little fat Frog to go to hell with his admiration," he squawked. "Admiration leads to covetousness, and covetousness is a sin that leads to theft." And he shook a broken-handled hoe at us.

"He is insolent. He presumes upon his years, that old miserable," Monsieur de Saint Loup commented as we turned away. His smile and shrug were indulgent; but his face, I observed with astonishment, was again dark crimson, as it had been when he quelled little Aggie Van Zile's cur. This intensity of feeling at so trivial a cause annoyed me somehow so that I made no reply but turned and waved to the miser in farewell.

How strange it has seemed to me since then to think that as I turned away from him that afternoon I had within my knowledge all the factors with which to explain the fantastic and terrible happenings which were to leave me but a few

8

weeks later with my hair whitened at the temples and my right arm limp and all but useless for the rest of my life!

"A happy country," Monsieur de Saint Loup was saying with a return to his usual manner, when I next gave him my attention. "A happy country where a feeble old man can live alone in so secluded a spot with all his wealth about him! He does live alone, I am to understand?"

I answered that it would take more money than old Peter would be willing to pay to hire anybody to live with him.

"In Europe he would have his feet burned some night with red-hot irons until either he divulged his hoard or died of the torture," said Monsieur de Saint Loup.

II. — COUSIN FELICITY

Small as the incident was, it had robbed me of the pleasure I had been taking in the society of my companion. In the tone of his last remark there had been a kind of zest ill-suited to the words. as if old Peter's boorishness still rankled in him and the thought of him in agony gave him a perverted enjoyment. I began to wish that with decency I could conduct him back to his lodgings by the way by which we had come, and be rid of him. I remembered work at the office which I would have been glad to finish before closing time, and I recalled what had never been far from my conscious thought all day, the fact that my Cousin Felicity, as my uncle called her, might well arrive from Maryland that afternoon.

There was in fact no tie of blood between her and me. The only child of his deceased wife's brother — her mother dead at her birth and her father some six months ago — my uncle had written at once to offer her a home with him, and in the meanwhile had not failed to improve each opportunity with hints which it would have been hard to misunderstand. He expected us to marry, this unknown girl and me. And through us the Barclay blood, if not the Barclay name, was to carry on that business which, through a long and childless widowhood, had become to him like the flesh of his flesh and the bone of his bone. Boylike, I was about to write — but where is the man of any age who is prepared to fall in love with the woman whom another has chosen for him? With all the innate romance of a lad of twenty-one who has had but little girls in his life, I had not the slightest intention of permitting my young love to be so summarily disposed of. Was it likely, I asked myself, moreover, with what I took to be considerable shrewdness, that a pretty girl with a sweet disposition and engaging manners should have need of an uncle to find a husband for her?

So while I was leading Monsieur de Saint Loup along a

footpath that wound through slanting pastures and under the laden boughs of orchards down to the river level, I was asking myself whether she might not already have arrived, and the hundred other questions which that suggested. The rays of the fast-declining sun shot beneath the apple trees, touching our hands and faces with a fugitive warmth, but already the evening chill was rising from the river, and made a heady mixture with the scent of ripened fruit and the salty tang of the uprushing tide. The shadows of the hills of the western shore lay more than half across the stream. Far down its course the headlands, their summits still in strong sunshine, rose from a mysterious obscurity. The chimney pots of the town smoked with supper fires, and the weather-cock on Saint Michael's steeple flashed in its new gilding above the bristle of the leafless elm tree tops. The air was so still one could almost believe one heard the bickering of the current against the mole a good half-mile away. The town clock struck the hour.

If such a thought could have entered my mind, how impossible it would have seemed that by another evening terror should have begun to stalk through that abode of peace, that this was the last sunset for many weeks, through which men would stroll as we were strolling, without fear, and not go hurrying with backward glances and an eye that measured the approach of twilight and the distance to the nearest refuge!

From the post road carriage wheels grated on a ledge. A coachman's whip sent an echo crackling like a pistolshot. A light traveling-carriage rumbled up the road as we crossed the stile over the bordering wall. Its yellow panels shone in the sun; an old man with brass buttons to his coachman's coat of many capes, held the reins over two weary horses; a waiting-woman, a stately negress of middle-age, in a white turban and a red shawl pinned crosswise over her deep bosom, sat erect in the rumble. Two small leather trunks and a hamper on the luggage rack confirmed the impression made by the servants, and when a young girl leaned across the lowered glass of the door to ask if it was indeed New Dortrecht just ahead, I had no need of her Southern accent to make me sure.

This was the young person whom I had schooled myself silently and stubbornly to dislike in advance, who might be as pretty and engaging as my uncle promised, but if she were, must then conceal some fault of disposition or character that should justify the prejudice which I entertained against her. And now that I found her a young beauty who emphasized the gentle and unaffected dignity with which she put her question with a frank, straight look of quiet self-possession, each natural inclination drove my prejudice to the winds, trampled on my resolution and threw me into such complete disorder

10

that I stood for the moment dumb.

Monsieur de Saint Loup suffered from no such disadvantage. Hat in hand, he spoke at once with all of his racial volubility. Did he comprehend the nature of Mademoiselle's question? Had she inquired the way? Would she be good enough to ask the question again, and slowly, so that a poor foreigner like himself might be sure of understanding it? I came to myself to find him ogling her with those tawny eyes of his as I had seen the gallants of the boulevards ogle the ladies of the Palais Royal. Her color was rising under his gaze; her fine brows, duskily golden, drew together ever so slightly; and she stammered a little as she began to repeat her inquiry. My blood boiled.

"Pardon, Monsieur," I said brusquely. "This lady is my affair." And I stepped in front of him. A Frenchman would be a Frenchman, of course, but if he would not learn the manners of the country he desired to adopt, he must be taught — that was all.

"But I think not," he was for breaking in.

"She is Miss Paige from Maryland, my cousin, whom my uncle has been expecting this week past," I went on decisively, placing myself between him and her in such a way that my words could not possibly be construed as an introduction. Then, turning, I laid my hand upon the carriage door.

"I am Robert Farrier, Cousin Felicity. If you will allow me, I will get in and direct your coachman to our Uncle Barclay's house."

I leaned from the window to speak again to Monsieur de Saint Loup: "You will excuse me, I am sure, sir, in the circumstances. You have but to follow this road to reach the High Street and your lodgings. My uncle has promised himself the pleasure of waiting on you after supper. Au revoir."

"I shall be charmed by the attention," he replied civilly enough; and off we drove, leaving him, still hat in hand, by the roadside. But his face wore again the same smoldering red which I had already seen twice that afternoon. It was not on me, however, that his glance lingered. He appeared to be staring at something on the carriage, something at one side and a little above me. I leaned out, craning my neck as far as possible, to see what it might be that so greatly interested him, and so managed to catch a glimpse of Felicity's waiting-woman. With her vigorous torso twisted half around in the rumble, the strong, clean line of jaw and chin sharp against the evening sky, she seemed to be staring back at him.

"You have come far today, Cousin Felicity?" I asked, as I settled back upon the seat. At her side, in the small compass of the carriage, I felt my head beginning to whirl again.

11

"Not above fifteen miles, I think, Cousin Robert," she answered demurely, her curved lashes almost touching her softly flushed cheeks. "We drove upwards of thirty yesterday; so we rested the horses and started late today."

"They are the same horses with which you left Maryland, Cousin Felicity?"

"The very same, Cousin Robert." But now her lashes were up; her eyes laughed at me; and the soft curves of her lips broke into a smile that set a dimple coming and going in her left cheek. "Yes, Cousin. Also the roads were excellent in the main, and I thought Philadelphia a prodigious great town, but New York livelier. The weather was favorable; I was never unduly fatigued, and — "

"Here, here!" I laughed, catching the spirit of her mockery. "If you proceed to squander our subject matter like this, how are we to sustain a conversation till we reach our uncle's house?"

"Tell me about that dreadful little Frenchman," she begged, and became suddenly so grave that I was struck by the thoughtful beauty of her face, which her animation had masked with mere prettiness. "He cannot be as bad as the impression which he made upon me, I suppose, or he would not have been in your company; my uncle would not be calling upon him this evening. But what is he?"

I told her the little that I knew, adding that she must not judge a Frenchman by manners which he had not yet learned were out of place with us.

"Oh," she shrugged, "it was not that. But there was something horrible about him. Perhaps it was those long teeth: they go so ill with his pudgy round body. And the way he flushed and glared when you turned to get into the carriage and he saw that you did not intend to present him to me! I should be on my guard against him, Cousin Robert. He felt himself deeply affronted, and I am sure he knows how to be dangerous," she added seriously.

"Perhaps your waiting-woman thinks as you do," said I. "Either that or Monsieur de Saint Loup has taken her fancy."

"Oh, Vashti! She spent her girlhood in Hayti, saw her mother flogged to death, poor creature. She hates all Frenchmen on principle. But I mean what I say about this man, Cousin Robert. I never got such a peculiar and unpleasant impression from anybody, and he was deeply offended."

"And I meant only to teach him a lesson in American manners," I said gaily, and opened the door. For the carriage drew up before our uncle's house just then, and Uncle Barclay, returning home from the business of the day, was in the act of

12

mounting the shallow steps of scrubbed white stone that led up from the brick footpath between curving iron railings to his front door. I caught a single swift impression of weariness from his lowered head and stooping shoulders before he saw us. But he was altogether his usual erect and stately self as he turned at sound of our halt and descended. I saw Felicity bestow one startled glance at the wide-skirted coat and wig which he continued to wear in spite of changing fashions since people told him he looked like President Washington in them. He made her welcome in one of his carefully formed phrases and enfolded her in a paternal embrace, then turned to greet her servants and commend them to the guidance of Barry, his trusted butler and valet, who hurried down the steps to direct the disposal of the luggage. But Felicity was quick to sense the real warmth of affection, the fundamental kindness, that lay beneath this pompous show. She was amused, I suspected, instead of being chilled, or made merely contemptuous, as almost any other girl would have been; and her gay acquiescence in her ceremonious investiture as chatelaine of our uncle's house — for his course and manner both at supper and afterwards were such as to justify the phrase — appeared to suit him exactly.

He did not make his promised call on Monsieur de Saint Loup that evening, but with Felicity's lovely face and fair young shoulders glowing softly in the light of the silver candlesticks across the dark mahogany of the supper table he sent off a note of excuse; and I don't know which was pleasanter to see, his restrained delight in having a feminine presence once more presiding at his lonely board, or the spontaneous friendliness and delicate tact with which the young girl assumed each of her new duties at the very moment when he would have had her do so.

After supper, amid the somewhat musty elegance of the dim old drawing-room, which had been unlocked and made ready against her coming only the week before, she fastened a bit of work to the long-disused embroidery frame beside the hearth and made him laugh with tales of the mischances of her journey. Presently he gave her the key to the harpsicord, which for so many years had been but the gorgeous red and black and gold sarcophagus of music, and sat motionless, with a gentle smile on his vain, handsome face, while she plucked from the neglected wires a plaintive accompaniment to the melodies of the South.

When Barry brought in the usual decanter of rum, hot-water jug, sugar and lemons at half-past nine, it was before her that he set the tray. She said that it had always been her task to mix her father's toddy at home, but we must give her

13

minute directions tonight, for she had never seen two
gentlemen who liked it the same. She praised Barry for the
exceeding hotness of the water and dismissed him with a smile.

I like to remember all these little things about the happiness
of that first evening. It ended just there, almost in that very
moment, and never returned to all three of us again for many
weeks. Felicity arose with my uncle's steaming glass in her
hand — "No," she told me, "I must be the one to give it to
him tonight." She almost reached him, when suddenly she
gave a low scream; her hands flew to her breast; the glass
shivered on the waxed boards of the floor; and she swayed, her
eyes wide with terror and fixed on one of the long French
windows at the end of the room.

I sprang for that, for my uncle had already caught her in his
arms. By some oversight the heavy red damask curtains had
not been drawn fully across it, but to my startled glance the
panes gave back no more than a bright and confused reflection
of the room. I wrenched the long sash open and made a swift
examination of the little high-walled garden without, but
could make no guess at what had so greatly terrified her. When
I returned to the room she was so far recovered as to have
begun a laughing apology for her conduct.

"I am very much mortified, Uncle Barclay," I heard her
say. "You will think me quite mad, but I thought I saw a great
wolf looking in through that window. Do you keep an
enormous hound on watch at night, or must I conclude that I
am more fatigued by my journey than I was aware of?"

"I keep no dog of any sort, nor could any dog get over my
walls out there," my uncle began in a puzzled tone, his eyes
ranging about the room as if in search of an answer to the
riddle. Then he laughed, walked halfway to the window and
kicked up with his foot the gaping head of a fine black
bearskin rug. "From just where you stood you must have
caught some exaggerated reflection of that in the pane and,
fatigued as you doubtless are, your imagination did the rest.
Let us demonstrate. Robert, the curtain. Draw it back again."

"No, No!" cried the girl. "Of course you are right. Cousin
Robert would have been bitten into shreds if what I saw had
really been out there. But I don't want to see those eyes again.
They seemed to glare directly at me."

Her agitation was so genuine that my uncle did not press
the point; and indeed it seemed impossible that there could be
any other explanation for what she thought she had seen than
the one he had hit upon. No wolf had been heard of within
twenty miles of New Dortrecht since one of those terrible
winters of the Revolutionary War, when the depredations of
the Indians along the frontier had let the terrors of the

wilderness in upon us. Mr. Sackville kept a great mastiff, but it never roamed about alone. Moreover, as my uncle said, his garden walls, topped with glass, made access impossible to any animal. So we drank our toddy; Felicity bade us good night; and I went home to my father's old house by the river, my mind too filled with her and all those once so well-hated plans of his to give another thought to the episode. I did wonder idly why all the dogs in town were barking furiously. But a moist breeze had sprung up. Doubtless it bore to them the scent of some prowling fox among the upland farms, thought I — until next morning.

Then I was awakened with the news that a farm laborer, making a short-cut through old Peter's garden at dawn, had found him dead on his back doorsteps with his throat in bloody tatters. The course of the beast that had wrought this horror — an enormous timber wolf, to judge by the shape and size of its tracks — could be followed in the dust of half the streets of the town. The animal must have ranged almost incredibly far from the wild fastnesses where alone it could enjoy any security of existence. But all the evidence appeared to debar any other conclusion. No wonder that the dogs had been astir! But that didn't make it any more likely that a wolf had been able to clear my uncle's walls.

III. — WOLF! WOLF!

I was later than many in hearing the dreadful news about old Armitage. But the sun was not yet over the little pine wood at the back of the place when I arrived there; and in its shadow the deep, tangled garden, the sodden masses of withered flower-stalks, still glistening with the moisture of the night, showed with a kind of lugubrious clarity. Although the gap in the rear wall, which had afforded the early laborer who found the body so tempting a short-cut to his work, was years old, its fallen stones and jagged edges gave an unpleasant suggestion of recent violence, as if it, too, had been the work of the bestial marauder. And anything of grisly significance which the scene might have lacked for one ignorant of what had lately happened there was supplied by the low-voiced, excited little groups that stamped about, staring at the great wolf tracks in the soft earth of the paths and shunning, for the most part, the dark red stains that greased the stone steps of the little porch outside the kitchen door.

The body had been carried inside, where the coroner and the sheriff himself were in consultation over it; and I had no sooner mentioned my last sight of the old man on the previous afternoon than Jake Dunkard, the constable, who had been assigned to protect the traces of the outrage from careless sight-seers, asked me to go in and tell what I knew. If the garden was depressing, the kitchen was downright dismal with the cold light of its single window falling on the rough board floor and the walls of cracked plaster patched and streaked with the brown and green of damp and mildew. An odor of unventilated sleep and stale bedding pervaded the air. Yet as I looked down upon the late owner of this squalid place, lying stark and stiff on the worn deal of his kitchen table, his almost fleshless shanks and knotty feet sticking out from beneath a short, blood-stained nightshirt, and observed his cup and plate with the knife and spoon laid ready where he had placed them the night before, a sudden pity gushed within me. He looked so small and fragile, so incapable of doing any great harm to anyone; and it seemed so pitifully absurd that all those years of stern self-abnegation should have brought him at last to be no more than a common gazing-stock, a public horror at which men felt neither regret nor grief, about whom the sheriff was already fuming to be gone and little Doctor Van Ryn evidently meant to manufacture for himself the greatest possible importance.

To my surprise I found the Reverend Mr. Sackville with the two officers. But from his answers to the questions which they were putting to him I soon understood the reason for his presence there. An early riser by habit, he had gone to his garden door to call in his great mastiff to keep him company at breakfast as he was used to do. He had found the magnificent animal dead, slain by a single huge bite which had broken the backbone just behind the skull. He had heard no unusual sounds during the night, except that the dog had barked from time to time — but all the dogs in town seemed to have been doing that. There had been no struggle, only a noiseless leap from behind. The single wound and the tracks in the soft earth of the flower-beds showed that.

All this while, you may be sure, I was not forgetful of Felicity's fright in my uncle's drawing-room. Was our explanation of it wrong? Might not this great beast have cleared the garden wall? But if it had, why should such a savage creature have fled at my mere opening of the window? I did not mention the occurrence, however, when my turn came to be questioned. Van Ryn annoyed me too much, and I determined that he should not have the chance to display his authority by badgering my lovely cousin with his absurd questions. He was like some ghastly showman as he snatched the slazy square of dishcloth which covered them from old Peter's face and breast and called on me to identify the 'murdered man' as the one whom I had seen and talked with in front of the house on the previous afternoon. If it had been

16

possible to believe that anything but the jaws of a ferocious animal had made that ragged gash, you might have supposed from his questions and his manner of putting them that he suspected me of doing it.

Did I go inside the gate during my conversation with old Peter? Had I been alone with him? I am sure he was disappointed to learn that Monsieur de Saint Loup had been with me throughout and that I had not left his side. Van Ryn was about to summon him in hot haste, when the door opened and Monsieur de Saint Loup appeared in lively altercation with Jake Dunkard, who endeavored to prevent his entrance.

My first thought was that the Frenchman was in a state of suppressed excitement. His face had lost all its ruddiness; there were deep circles under his eyes; and there seemed to me to be something like covert eagerness in the quick glances with which he took in the room and its occupants. The uncompromising light of the early morning and the shocking circumstances of the occasion were quite enough to account for all this, however. He was as scrupulously dressed and shaven as on the previous afternoon, and his features, taken without the restless eyes, wore a look of seriousness of which I should not have supposed them capable. He bore steadily the ordeal of examining the dreadful sight upon the table, as he was called upon to do, and answered all questions with remarkable directness and address, I thought, considering that he was using a language foreign to him.

But I had been given something else to think about before the coroner had finished with him. I felt the nudge of an elbow in my side and looked up to find the shrewd old eyes of the rector leading mine to the table. Unwillingly I looked, and looked again, but could not guess what he was driving at. A slow ooze of blood from the wound was the only change I noted there. It turned out, as I might have expected, to be only another of those queer darts of fancy with which his delvings into the bypaths of historical research were continually inspiring him. I heard all about it as I walked down the hill with him and Monsieur de Saint Loup after the coroner had dismissed us. Meanwhile I was amused and interested by the contrast between those two: the short round figure of the Frenchman, all volubility and gesture, and Mr. Sackville's six-feet-three of gaunt strength which seventy years of age and seven of persecution, while his ordination vows kept him loyal to George III, had failed to bow, the gleaming silver of the thick hair that fell to his shoulders, the bright spots of healthy color on his high cheek bones, and the dry humorous quirk of his lips before he put the following question:

17

"Did it occur to you, Monsieur, that if we had been in France, or indeed anywhere in Europe, in the Middle Ages, your position up there in old Armitage's kitchen would have been decidedly uncomfortable?"

"My position uncomfortable – in the Middle Ages – if we were there just now? I do not think I have thought of the Middle Ages while I was in that kitchen, Mr. Sackville. I thought all was very characteristic of this new, free country in these modern times. You should see such a thing in France – the police, the officials, the uniforms, the what you call red tape. This officer, if a little pompous, a little absurd, was evidently honest, reasonably direct." Monsieur de Saint Loup paused as if he had finished with what he had to say, then added civilly; "But you, it appears, sir, did think something about the Middle Ages. What was it? You interest me."

"I meant the behavior of the body," Mr. Sackville replied gravely, though I caught the twinkle in his blue eyes beneath their bushy brows. "The wound bled afresh when you stooped over it. In the Middle Ages they would have hanged you as high as Haman on that evidence alone, if I understand my reading of those times correctly. Am I right?"

The Frenchman shrugged. He thought he had read something of the kind, he said indifferently. But his tone made it clear that he also thought the clergyman's remarks were in abominable taste. What with the gusto with which Mr. Sackville had brought them out, I myself did not relish them – much as I liked him – so soon after the scene of mortality which we had just quitted. And I wondered at his making them, for in spite of his downright honesty and directness he was peculiarly sensitive to the fitness of things. It immediately appeared that he too was aware of having transgressed the limits of so brief an acquaintance. In his very next words he moderated his manner and with the charming courtesy characteristic of him begged permission to call upon Monsieur de Saint Loup that afternoon and the pleasure of his company to dinner the next day week.

The Frenchman was quick to accept the implied apology and the invitation as well; and, to make it quite clear apparently that he harbored no ill-feeling about the clergyman's untimely speech, he went on to say:

"I gather that witchcraft is not the only superstition that interests you, sir."

"Our friend Farrier here has been telling you of that weakness of mine, has he?" Mr. Sackville replied with a smile.

"He gave me to understand that you believe that there may actually have been such a thing, that its practitioners were not all necessarily either frauds or lunatics, and that there may still be people alive who possess such supernatural powers."

Mr. Sackville gave him a keen look at that, as if to be sure that the other was not making game of him.

"It is difficult to be certain that any evil thing has been exterminated absolutely. Consider the tragedy of this very morning. Last night the oldest inhabitant of this neighborhood would have assured you that there wasn't a timber wolf left within a hundred miles of us, that there couldn't be; and now I leave you to officiate at the funeral of my good four-footed friend Nero who could have accounted for any two ordinary wolves. You observe the parallel which I would draw?"

We had reached the entrance to a bypath which, skirting the upper edge of the town, led to his back garden gate. He raised his hat and bowed, repeated his promise to call upon Monsieur de Saint Loup that afternoon and left us.

"I wish," said the latter, as we continued on down the hill, "that my wolfhound De Retz had been here and at large last night. Without disrespect to his Nero we should have had a different story to consider this morning had he encountered this marauder. I shall be glad to have him here in the future."

He parted from me at the door of my uncle's place of business, wishing, he said, to consult a lawyer; and I directed him to Squire Killian's office.

"I desire," he went on with a gleam of mischief in his eyes and that low mirthful growl, which I had not heard from him that morning until now, "I desire to learn about the American laws regarding the acquisition of property by an alien. I told you yesterday that I liked the house of that old miserable up there. I believe I said that I would have it. You remember, eh?"

"I remember also what he said about covetousness. Good morning, sir," I answered stiffly and, swinging myself around by the iron handrail, I stamped up the brick steps and slammed the door of the counting-house behind me. Old Peter hardly cold, there was something in his manner of speaking that outraged my sense of decency far more than the mere meaning of the words could have done.

My anger quickly subsided. I even saw that it had been foolish. Difference of customs, difference of language, easily accounted for the seeming heartlessness which had disgusted me. Determined to make amends for my rudeness at the first opportunity, I put the whole matter out of my mind. Other thoughts now arose, thoughts which even the exciting events of the morning had hardly sufficed to keep down. For I, who had never been more than mildly exhilarated by a pretty face, whose heart had never lost a beat at the smile of the loveliest girl that ever graced one of our winter assemblies, had fallen deep in love. Half the night I had tossed in my bed, listening to the interminable barking of the dogs, now down by the river, now from the outskirts to the north, and finally, not long before daylight, as it died away upon the hilltops. And I had awakened deeper in love than when I lay down.

I had climbed the hill to old Peter's, light-footed with exultation. I was shocked and perhaps honestly a little saddened by the cause of my going there — after all, the old man had never ceased to acknowledge in his churlish way the small kindness which I had done him so many years ago. But at heart I went rejoicing. For I saw the course of true love running straight and smooth before me, and I sang an inward song at the sight. But once on my high stool and bending over my work, as if my anger at Saint Loup had been a mysterious reagent, my joyous confidence gave place to despair. What mattered it that by a miracle my wishes coincided with my uncle's? Who was I that the loveliest girl in the created universe should look on me with favor? The memory of what had been my thoughts of her until yesterday, my repugnance toward the marriage of convenience which I felt sure that our uncle planned for us, mocked my hopes. Was it likely that she had been more unsuspecting of such an arrangement than I had been, or that she had found the project less unpleasing? Her mere appearance had been enough to revolutionize my feelings, of course. But what reason had I to suppose that hers had been changed?

A more horrid thought assailed me. Might not her affections be already possessed by some brilliant young Southerner who, although not yet prepared to marry, enjoyed such expectations as to permit him to enter upon an engagement? The idea tormented me all day and with such intensity that, as I walked homeward with my uncle at supper time according to our usual custom, I plumped out with it.

He gave his great, empty-sounding laugh.

"Probable? Yes. But not the fact. It happens that I have sounded her on that point."

"You have?" I could not help exclaiming.

"Why, yes. The thought of such a thing hadn't crossed my mind. But Saint Loup put it into my head, saying he supposed she was already betrothed to you."

"I should be very glad, sir," I said impulsively, "if that could be brought to pass."

"And I've no doubt you would," he replied drily. "My niece strikes me as fitted to be the wife of a man in the very highest station. Saint Loup was much impressed by her, though he saw her for only a moment in the carriage yesterday."

20

"That was evident," I returned with equal dryness, and I gave him a full account of the little Frenchman's behavior.

"Oh, these Frenchmen!" he remarked tolerantly. "A woman is a woman first with them, though she may prove to be a lady afterwards. Saint Loup is no fool by the way. Do you know what he did with his property — everything that wasn't entailed, that is — the moment the Bastille fell? Put it into British consols. Shrewd, eh? Remarkably shrewd for a noble, I call it."

We had reached his door by this time. For, although nothing had been said about my coming to supper, I had been so sure that such an invitation would be a part of his plans for Felicity and me that I had walked on with him past the corner where our ways should have separated. But he now held out his hand and bade me good night.

What with the agony of the thoughts which had tortured me all day, and the bewilderment with which I had just seen him smile away — for it seemed to me that he had done nothing less — the whole airy fabric on which I had built my feeble hopes, this disappointment seemed more than I could endure. I felt that I had to see Felicity that night, if it were only for a glance and a touch of her hand.

"If you will permit me, sir," I said boldly, "I should like to come in and glance about the garden. After hearing of this wolf's exploit at Mr. Sackville's I would like to make sure that our explanation of my cousin's fright last night was the true one."

"There can be no doubt of that," he replied. "But come in, if you like. You will excuse me if I go on up stairs at once."

He could have done nothing that I would have excused more willingly, especially as he did not so much as look in at the drawing-room door in passing. Felicity was there. At sight of her, her duskily golden head gleaming in the candlelight, her white hands poised above the embroidery frame as I entered, half my new anxieties were forgotten. The other half fled at the welcoming note in her voice. Let my uncle's wishes be what they might, she was pledged to no other.

"My dear Robert, I'm so glad you have come," she exclaimed; then, lowering her voice, "I've been making an experiment. I've something to show you. That was no reflection which I saw in the window last night. Look! The lights and curtains are exactly as they were then. Yet, stand where you will, you cannot see the head of that bearskin in the pane. The wolf that killed that old man was in our garden, and I saw him."

Her hand sought mine and grasped it.

"Horrors, Robert! Suppose he had fallen upon you when

you rushed out! If only you had seen him standing there, devouring me with his eyes! The thought of it sends a cold thrill down my spine now."

My body, too, was thrilling, but it was the warm clasp of her hand that made it do so. My fingers tightened over hers.

"Come," I said. "Let us each take a candle and search the garden for tracks. That is my excuse for being here."

"There are none. I looked this morning. And the walks are all of brick as you know; and one of them does lead directly to that window. But don't tell me you aren't staying for supper!" And the regret in her voice more than paid me for all my disappointment on that score.

"I'm not invited, my dear cousin," I told her. "It was not prearranged, and when you know our uncle better you will observe that he is not one to offer pot-luck."

"What a shame! If I had been here a month instead of only a day, I'd ask you on my own responsibility. However, you are invited tomorrow night. Don't tell me you cannot come, for I should never be able to support Monsieur de Saint Loup's presence without you."

"Monsieur de Saint Loup tomorrow night? There is nothing tardy about our uncle's hospitality, is there? You may be sure I will come. It would take more than he to keep me away, though I find that I like him no better than you do."

"Oh, but our uncle tells me that I am quite wrong in that." She made a delightful face. "He says what you did, that a Frenchman ogles every woman, and that actually Monsieur de Saint Loup is a man of ideas as sound as his finances, which, it appears, are excellent."

Her hand had continued to lie in mine, but the frank, cordial pressure she game me with it at parting showed how unconscious of any possible sentimental significance she was in letting it remain there. Lover-like, I was idiotic enough to allow this thought to rob the memory of our interview of half its charm. I was her cousin, whom she liked as a cousin very well, nothing more, I told myself bitterly as I walked to my own house and solitary supper there. I reminded myself that I had already played the fool quite sufficiently for one day, and I grew hot all over as I thought of the smile with which my uncle had heard me avow my willingness toward a betrothal with his niece. But what else could he have meant by all those weeks of hinting and sly nods? Or had he suddenly changed his mind? And if so, why? Because this ci-devant noble with his fortune in British consols had appeared on the scene and been impressed by the first sight of her? But I had not yet begun to realize how seriously the widespread financial depression of that summer had effected the old firm of Barclay and Barclay;

and I was too young to know how easy it is for a man of my uncle's temperament to make himself believe that he is acting on the most unselfish motives when he is serving his own interests.

IV. – LOVE MY DOG, LOVE ME

I was, of course, the perfect prey for jealousy when I presented myself at my uncle's house for supper the following evening. And if Felicity gave me no cause for indulging that contemptible passion – as I must acknowledge that she did not – Monsieur de Saint Loup afforded me plenty of excuses. I have said that for all his air of jovial chubbiness he did not lack a certain distinction and, when he chose, an adequate dignity. Dressed for the evening with a costly and unobtrusive elegance, the exquisite lace at his throat fastened by a magnificent ruby, and in his hand a snuffbox of fine enamels, he presented a changed appearance, a manner subtly altered.

By candle-light his face seemed to have lost the warm flush that suggested by daylight an excess of animal spirits. It was only when one stood close to him that one could see the tiny globules of sweat beading the dark blue surface of his shaven upper lip. The tawny lights in his black eyes gave them a look of melancholy. The cunning lines of a coat of claret colored satin concealed the plumpness of his figure. He might know as little of Paris as he pretended, but no provincial tailor had cut that coat.

I had looked forward, meanly enough, to seeing him a little cheapened in contrast with the appointments of my uncle's dining room. Instead, the fine napery, the old massive silver and crystal, took on in his presence a look of mere adequacy, of being good of their kind but no more than what a gentleman like him would expect.

Gone was his bubbling good humor. He maintained an urbanity rather grave than otherwise, even when Felicity had left us to our wine. In the drawing-room afterwards he bore himself toward her with a kind of lofty and wistful humility which made me want to kick him but which was quick to wipe away the unpleasant impression he had made when she first saw him. He was on his feet to lead her to the harpsicord the moment that my uncle suggested that she sing for us, and within five minutes he was bending with her over the music of a duet. In ten they appeared to have forgotten the rest of us, my uncle, the rector, who was the only other guest, and me, while they enlivened brief trials of this song and that with bursts of talk in a French too rapid for me to follow.

"A strange fellow," commented Mr. Sackville, when it became clear that they were bent only on amusing themselves.

23

"Civil enough, interesting, but with something — something tropical about him that makes my northern blood simmer. I cannot say I like him."

"I have found him a man of singularly sound ideas for these days," my uncle replied calmly, "by no means blindly devoted to the old order of things but absolutely unsympathetic with the excesses of the present day."

"So he informed me," said Mr. Sackville. Evidently he recognized the tone which my uncle was in the habit of using to terminate a discussion which he regarded as useless before it was well begun, and he abruptly changed the subject.

"There was one curious thing about old Armitage's death, Mr. Barclay, which was not brought out at the inquest this afternoon. You may have noticed it, Robert. Doubless it has no practical bearing on the case; but I kept asking myself what induced old Peter to come out into his garden at such an hour. It is notorious that the house was locked up like a prison at all times, especially at night, and that he would never come out of doors between darkness and dawn — not even the night of the great fire years ago, when blazing brands alighted on his roof. Now I am idle enough to wonder why he came out night before last. Had the question occurred to either of you?"

"Eh? Er — I beg your pardon, sir." My uncle stammered as if he had fallen into so deep a reverie that he had failed to gather what the clergyman had said. "That is to say, sir, have you arrived at any solution," he recovered himself.

"Only a poor one," Mr. Sackville replied. "And that is based on the vulgar superstition that the poor wretch's garden is sown with buried treasure. If we accept that, it is possible he mistook some sound made by the wolf for that of a person moving about in search of it."

"Pooh!" returned my uncle. "I doubt if he had a hundred dollars to his name; and if he had, he was too shrewd to bury it. You know how a small town will talk about any old man who lives solitary and makes himself thoroughly disagreeable to everybody. It seems to me that probably he was taken with some sudden illness and attempted to seek a physician."

"In his nightshirt? He had on nothing else."

"Ah?" said my uncle. "I hadn't heard that detail. I happen to have had two most absorbing days at my office and have given so little attention to the affair that — Now that is charming, is it not?" he broke off as after two or three false starts interspersed with Felicity's laughter the two at the harpsicord began to sing.

Monsieur de Saint Loup had an excellent baritone voice and used it cunningly as a foil for the prettiness of my cousin's drawing-room soprano. Song followed song in response to the

24

hearty applause of my uncle and the rector, and more and more often I saw Felicity turn to the Frenchman a face flushed with pleasure at the entirety of their accord. It was a sour smile I gave them, I fear, when at last he led her towards us and bowed, while she swept a curtsy, as if they had been professional performers.

"Since you deign to be pleased by our music, sir," said he, "Mademoiselle would ask a boon in my behalf. She has undertaken to shelter my poor hound until I can prepare proper quarters for him. She begs for him the hospitality of your stable until that time."

Felicity explained. It appeared that Monsieur de Saint Loup must go to New York within a week to see about forwarding his effects and, having a good deal of other business to transact there, wished to send these along ahead of his return and his dog with them. To find a proper guardian and lodging for the animal had perplexed him.

"De Retz is a peculiar creature, slow to become acquainted with strangers," Monsieur de Saint Loup appended, adding with a smile and a bow in the right direction, "unless they happen to be charming young ladies."

"I do not see why the animal cannot have one of the empty loose-boxes in my stable," said my uncle. "But tell me, sir. You have already found quarters here that suit you?"

"Squire Killian tells me that I may have the house of poor old Mr. Armitage." I caught a side glint of triumph directed at me from the Frenchman's eyes as he spoke. "It will be informal at first, but one which he feels quite sure can be made regular."

"You aren't afraid of treasure-hunters or ghosts either, I take it," Mr. Sackville commented.

"Not with De Retz at my side."

"De Retz? A curious name that for a dog." One saw the rector's interest quicken. "It is not so inappropriate for a wolfhound now that I think of it. But you must have had Gilles de Laval's early life in mind when you gave it to a favorite dog, I suppose."

By their faces I saw that this remark was as far beyond my uncle and Felicity as it was beyond me. Monsieur de Saint Loup, however, seemed to catch its bearing, for he replied quickly:

"Nay, sir. I had not the Sire de Retz in mind at all. It was the Cardinal, the Frondeur of that name, I was thinking of. His memories fascinate me."

"Indeed," said the rector, and gave his hearty laugh. "I ask your pardon and your dog's also." Then, observing our puzzled faces, he made haste to explain. "Gilles de Laval, Sire de Retz, was a comrade-in-arms of Joan of Arc and a Marshal of France, a man of holy life, but he ended by being strangled and burnt for murdering little children. He was accused of lycanthropy, was he not, Monsieur de Saint Loup?"

"Very likely, Mr. Sackville." The Frenchman's tone seemed to verge upon the insolent in its indifference. "It is the Cardinal de Retz that interests me."

"And aren't any of you gentlemen going to tell a poor, ignorant girl from the South what lycanthropy is? That is to say, if it isn't something too improper for her to ask about," begged Felicity.

"Monsieur de Saint Loup should be the best able to do that," said the rector, to whom her glance had appealed. "The history of his native province is filled with instances of lycanthropy. Will you not chill our blood with some old fireside tale of werewolves?"

"The subject has never interested me," replied the Frenchman. "I am sorry, Mademoiselle, but I have always regarded those old tales as rather tiresome."

"Werewolf doesn't help you?" Mr. Sackville asked of her, when she had expressed her disappointment. "Well, a lycanthropist is no more than the French Canadian Loup-garou turned into Greek."

"But Maryland is so far from Canada, Mr. Sackville," she lamented, "that I'm no better off than I was before."

"Then I see that I must hold forth. But your uncle won't like it, for it's a part of that old hobby of mine, and it bores him as much as I fear it will bore this good gentleman from Auvergne."

I glanced at Monsieur de Saint Loup at this, and it seemed that for a man who expected to be bored he was giving Mr. Sackville an extraordinary degree of attention.

"Lycanthropy in our modern sense means only a form of insanity," Mr. Sackville went on. "The unfortunate imagines that he is a wolf, and acts accordingly, if he is not restrained. But in the days of Gilles de Laval, the Sire de Retz, and all through the centuries when witchcraft and magic were believed in, it meant the assumption by a human being of the form and nature of a wolf. The power could be acquired, as such powers so often were, by selling one's soul to the Devil. But lycanthropy was also contagious. One bitten by a werewolf, which is the commonest name for the monster, became a werewolf. I could tell some terrible stories — "

"Spare us, good sir." Monsieur de Saint Loup had risen to his feet, smiling and holding out his hand to my uncle in farewell. "If you go on, you will recall my childhood, which was made frightful by such legends." And he proceeded to bid

26

my uncle good night and to thank him for his hospitality with all the effusiveness one expects from one of his nation. There was a deal of courtly parade in the way he kissed Felicity's hand, but he put a good deal more than courtly fervor into the pressure of his lips I guessed by the sudden, quick lifting of those golden brows of hers and the color that flooded her from breast to forehead; and I could have ground my teeth with vexation at the way in which my uncle practically made him free of the house at all hours when he expressed the hope that they might be at leisure to receive him again before his departure for New York.

"And while I shall be gone" — Monsieur de Saint Loup turned in the doorway, all his wistfulness departed and bold gaiety in the glance he directed at Felicity — "you have a proverb in English, I think — 'Love my dog, love me,' is it not?"

"Not exactly," she laughed. " 'T is love me, love my dog."

"Then I shall remind you of another," he countered. "It is a poor rule that does not work both ways." And even after the door had closed behind him I fancied that I heard the deep growl of his mirth.

"And now pray tell us some of those stories which he was afraid to listen to," Felicity exclaimed eagerly.

"My dear child, some other night." The rector was on his feet and took her hand to bid her farewell. "It is late and I must begin next Sunday's sermon before I go to bed. Shall I preach on Jeremiah, the Fifth Chapter and the sixth verse: 'A wolf of the evenings shall spoil them?' "

But she followed him to the door with her questions, at once scared and fascinated like a child. Were people supposed actually to change into wolves? How was that managed? He replied that they were believed to do it by turning the skin inside out; that the Romans called a werewolf versipellis, skin-changer; but there was no record of any witness who pretended to have actually seen such a transformation. The hair of the wolf was supposed to be on the under side of the skin when a werewolf wore his human form, and poor wretches accused of lycanthropy were often half skinned alive by the torturers in the attempt to prove its existence.

"And there were many of these creatures? I mean, there were believed to be?"

"In every country where there were wolves the belief in them was general. We spoke of the Sire de Retz. He was convicted of drinking the blood of little children. That was in 1440. In the Seventeenth Century a Hungarian countess used to torture young girls and bathe in their blood. They seem to have been especially fond of beautiful young girls. And now

27

good night, my children. I have talked too much. You will both have nightmares," he smiled with a shake of his snowy locks. We had both followed him out into the hall, and she had helped him to don his old-fashioned horseman's cloak and handed him his silver-tipped ebony staff as he finished speaking. He bowed to her with kindly ceremony.

"What a charming old man! What an altogether delightful evening!" she exclaimed, aglow with pleasure. "Who would expect to find two such interesting men in a remote little place like this?"

"Especially the fat little Saint Loup, I suppose," I returned like the lout jealousy had made of me. "I noticed that it didn't take him long to change the opinion you formed of him day before yesterday."

"But, Robert, he was so different tonight!"

"It didn't take you long to observe the difference."

"But he was our uncle's guest, to begin with. I had to be at least civil to him. And almost at once I saw that I had misjudged him. Nobody could have been more gentlemanlike or — "

"Or kissed your hand with a chillier respect?" I sneered, whipping up my anger with the memory of it. But at that she laughed outright.

"Robert, what of it? He's old enough to be my father. Don't tell me you are trying to be jealous — you, my cousin!"

"Jealous?" I cried; and then I said and did what fools like me, with thick black hair and blue eyes and great frames and muscles so heavy that we seldom use up half our strength, so often say and do: I made an idiot of myself both by speech and action. For the sense of her mocking beauty went over me like a fire. "I'm not your cousin. I only happen to be your uncle's nephew. And I thank God for it, for I love you, Felicity. And that wretch is a noble — a count, if he had his rights — and talented and rich, while I am a poor country clown without a thousand dollars to my name — "

Long before I had done speaking I had her in my arms, her pliant body crushed to mine, my words gasped out between the kisses with which I ravaged her sweet lips, her burning cheeks and fragrant hair.

"At worst," she panted, tearing herself out of my arms, "at worst, even you cannot imagine him treating me like this. I can only be glad that, as you remind me, you are not my cousin."

One might have counted ten, I suppose, while we stood confronting each other — if I could be said to confront her when I only slouched against the wall, where her final push had sent me. From a merry girl she had changed into an angry young woman, whose fingers might tremble at mending the

28

disorder of her hair, but whose eyes were clouded with her sense of outrage and — what was far worse for me — with disappointment in one whom she had taken for a friend. Then there came the skurry of feet in a perfect frenzy of haste on the flags without; the front door flew open; and the rector, hatless, his cloak rent and trailing, his staff a splintered fragment in his hand, sprang into the hall, slammed the door behind him and flung himself against its panels.

"The wolf," he gasped as he shot the bolt, and upon the word came the thud of might paws, the rattle of talons. The stout fabric shook under the impact of the weight hurled against it.

Mr. Sackville bent until his ear was at the keyhole, listened and raised his flushed face to grin at us.

"Lying in wait for me behind the bushes in my own front garden. One might say that the creature knew that I was out. Had the gate swung shut behind me instead of sticking, he would have had me for a certainty. Fortunately I was able to fling it to as I fled. He ran his nose against it: he was so close at my heels. It made him see stars, I fancy, and that gave me just the start I needed." He paused for a breathless laugh. "I don't believe I ever ran faster when I was a youth at King's College. Robert, do you suppose your uncle would lend me one of his double-barrelled pistols with which to make a second attempt to reach my fireside?"

"I'll go with you," I offered, only too glad of the opportunity to escape, for I was ashamed and disgusted with myself to a degree that made it impossible to frame an apology that night.

"Then you also must be armed." Felicity spoke with quick solicitude. I shot her a glance, grateful and amazed.

"Cousin," she added disdainfully.

V. – MISSING: A GREEN REDINGOTE

But now, his attention attracted by the slamming of the door and the sound of the rector's laugh, my uncle joined us in the hall and immediately vetoed so simple a solution of the affair as my escorting Mr. Sackville home, even though both of us should be armed. As one of the town councilors he felt the reappearance of the marauding beast to be a blot upon the administration in which he had a part. A reward of twenty-five dollars had been posted for the creature's hide. Hunters had scoured the neighborhood all day without success. The watch had been doubled — though it was whispered about that this was because every one of the three members of the force had refused point-blank to go on night duty alone.

What were the rascals about this evening, my uncle would

have liked to know. If he caught them boozing or shirking he would have their halberds and lanterns taken from them before midnight, though he went on guard in their place and swore in Barry and me as deputies, he fumed. He snatched from above the door the musket which he had shouldered under Abercrombie at Ticonderoga in his youth, tried the flint, rammed home a charge topped with slugs and primed the pan. Barry fetched a lantern and a fowling piece. I met Felicity's eyes, starry with excitement, and wondered that she showed no sign of uneasiness at being left alone. Then, upon the stairs behind her, I saw Vashti, her Haytian waiting-woman. Standing motionless, the whites of her eyes and her snowy turban alone relieving the darkness of her face and dress, she looked like some mysterious and powerful guardian spirit.

Barry drew the bolt; my uncle, his weapon ready, led us out; and at once the trail was hot before us. Where the beast had leapt against the door and slid down, foiled, its talons had furrowed the old layers of green paint from the breast-high brazen knocked almost to the threshold. The flagstones, glittering with hoarfrost in the lantern light, were sprinkled with the marks of the animal's great pads. In widely spaced clusters they showed where it had come leaping in pursuit; and we followed the regular pattern of the trot at which it had retired over the short distance to the High Street. There we lost all trace of it in the stiff rutted clay off the roadway.

"If only we had Monsieur's wolfhound," lamented my uncle, "we might at least learn the direction in which the brute went from here."

I can come close to laughter even now at the memory of those words, when I think of the part that wolfhound was to play in our search for this mysterious monster. I had much ado to keep from laughter, as it was, when we discovered both watchmen, halberds, lanterns and rattles, all complete, ensconced under the little portico of the town hall. The rector kept winking at me across the speckled illumination of the perforated lantern tops, and there was a strong flavor of Dogberry and Verges about the ensuing interview.

They were "just resting between rounds," Jake Dunkard explained. Not a beast had moved in the streets for an hour, excepting themselves and that new French gentleman, who had passed about an hour ago. They hadn't seen so much as a cat, let alone a wolf. My uncle heard them out in a disgusted silence, bade them follow him and proceeded to conduct us on a thorough patrol of the town. But not a trace of the animal could we discover. Even the dogs were silent, for no scent would carry far in that frosty night. A cold wind began to rush downward from the north, making the bare branches of the elm trees groan and clash as we went past the churchyard. There was no other sound but the clatter of our own feet in the echoing streets, until we encountered Monsieur de Saint Loup on his way down the road from old Peter Armitage's house, swinging a sheathed small-sword as if it were a walking stick and timing his steps to the whistle of a minuet. Mr. Sackville's remark concerning the possibility of treasure-seekers about the place had stirred his curiosity, he explained, and he had walked up there in the hope of surprising some of them in the garden. All had been quiet, however. When he understood our mission and my uncle had told them of Mr. Sackville's narrow escape, he shrugged with the amusement of a courageous man on hearing that he has been exposed to an unknown danger. He had seen no sign of our quarry, but he cheerfully enlisted under my uncle's leadership for the rest of the search.

It was almost one in the morning when we escorted him and the clergyman to their respective doors and from my front steps I watched my uncle and Barry as they tramped away to their own beds. My legs ached with weariness, but I could not sleep. Out of the darkness stared Felicity's outraged countenance as it had stared that long moment before Mr. Sackville burst in upon us in my uncle's hall. Worse still was the memory of the smile of humorous indulgence with which she had heard my jibes at her civility to the Frenchman a few minutes earlier. All day I had been telling myself how cheerfully I would die for her; and, lo, my love had proved too weak to bear the casual stresses of mere friendship. It had made a rogue of me — worse yet, a fool. For, poor as I was, I had my house; my employment gave me the means to dress as well as my station demanded and to keep a servant; I could look confidently to my uncle for advancement as fast as I deserved it; and Felicity, had I won her love, would have shared with joy the meager comforts I could offer. Of that I was sure. Yet I must needs throw this away and behave like a hopeless outlaw for no better reason than her common courtesy to my uncle's guest and his cool response to the proposal of myself to be her suitor!

Of course I told myself that I had ruined my cause for ever. Everything is final at twenty-two. And before I slept I had found solace in that last refuge of the self-confessed failure, a noble renunciation. My uncle knew no better than I did that Felicity was fitted to be the wife of a man in the very highest station. Should I, then, stand in the way of her marrying a rich man, a noble who could give her the position she was so well able to grace?

31

I was accordingly in no very hospitable state of mind when Squire Killian called on me before I had finished a tardy breakfast the following morning. A Yankee of the Yankees, he had been one of the few who had succeeded in establishing himself in New Dortrecht in face of the active prejudice of the original Dutch and English inhabitants against all members of that tide of shrewd and restless adventurers which had poured across the Berkshires after the Revolution and had already begun to dominate the country by means of their greater activity and enterprise. His honesty, intelligence and dry humor had made friends for him out of my uncle and the rector; and as usual the rest of the community had followed their lead. Lean, lantern-jawed, sententious to the point of affectation, he had that air of the pettifogger which seems so absurd to those who are too sophisticated to be impressed by it and at the same time too ignorant of a small-town lawyer's clientele to understand how essential it is to his success. So, since my return from my interrupted European travels, I had found his ponderous gravity and pretentions to a mysterious learning a little contemptible. I hadn't supposed that he was aware of this, however, until I caught a note of sarcasm in his apologies for interrupting me at my breakfast and indeed for troubling me at all with the concerns of his provincial practice.

I was young enough to be put a good deal out of countenance by this discovery, and I hastened to make such amends as I could, bidding Goody Hoskins set another chair and fetch hot muffins and fresh chocolate. Also I felt a strong curiosity as to how I might be so involved in anyone's affairs that I should be called upon by the lawyer at such an hour. He ate and drank almost without a word until my housekeeper had left the room. Then, wiping his lips with the back of one bony hand, he began.

"Old Armitage was quite a friend of yours, wasn't he? I mean, if he could be said to have a friend at all, you would be the one, wouldn't you?"

"If you put it that way," I assented.

"Never seemed to forget that small service you did him years ago? You needn't look surprised. I happened to see you do it, and I don't forget what I see."

"If he remembered it, he never mentioned it," I replied. "But at least he always spoke when we met, and spoke without cursing me, which was more than he often did to other people," I added, smiling.

"Ever talk to you about his will?"

"He never mentioned to me about anything."

"Ever mention his will?"

"Heavens, no! Did he leave one? I thought misers never did,

32

that they couldn't bear the thought of anybody else having their money even after they were dead."

"Never promised you anything — that you should get anything from him — after he was dead?"

"Good Lord, Squire," I exclaimed, somewhat nettled by this courtroom sort of interrogation, "if he had promised me anything worth while, do you think that in my circumstances I should have waited for you to come to me about it?"

"Your circumstances hardly strike me as desperate," the lawyer retorted, taking in with a look that was openly ironical the shabby coziness of the old, high-wainscoted room.

"My uncle and I have never believed that Armitage was worth more than a few hundred dollars, in any event," I went on with an air of superiority with which I intended to pay him off for his sarcasm. "Any old man of his sort, living as he did, is sure to have the reputation for fabulous hoarded wealth fastened upon him in a town of this size."

"Is he indeed?" The sparse gray hairs bristled as the lawyer pursed his lips unshaven since the previous morning. "Well, to be above vulgar gossip is very desirable — when one can afford it. And in this case it turns out to have cost you nothing either. But it happens that old Armitage died possessed of something like one hundred thousand dollars, unless I am much mistaken, and that I violate no canon of professional ethics by telling you so, for I believe you to be the sole legatee under his will."

"He did leave a will then?" I cried idiotically. But I was so amazed that I wonder I said anything at all.

"Aye, and left is just the word for what he did with it. The question is, where. Where did he leave it?"

"You mean that you don't know where it is, that it isn't in any of your strong boxes? Then how do you know — "

"I drew it, drew it last year soon after your return, about the time that the full extent of the ruin of your father's affairs became known. That's how I know."

"And he named me as his heir?"

"He did not. He named nobody, had me leave a space for the legatee's name, which he said he'd fill in for himself."

The lawyer, his wrinkled face for all the world like a shriveled pickle, sat grinning at me so exactly as if he could see my soaring hopes flutter to the ground that I grew hot with anger.

"I fear I must beg you to excuse me, Squire Killian," I said stiffly. "My duties at my uncle's counting-house will demand my presence there in a few minutes."

"And I will keep you but a few minutes more," he replied with as much gravity as if he had not just been amusing himself at my expense. "I have said that old Armitage had me leave the space blank but, walking over to the high clerk's desk where none could see what he wrote, he filled in the name. Then he folded that part of the instrument under and brought it back to my table and executed it, and old Sammy Rogers my clerk and I signed as witnesses."

"I see less and less how I can be concerned in the business," I was beginning, but he interrupted me with a kind of sour joviality, if I may so describe his manner.

"You shall, my young friend, and that immediately, for I am no more desirous of wasting time than you are. You shall have the most excellent reasons for being concerned in this business. Firstly, old Peter had been talking to me about drawing his will for years; and although he never told me whom he intended to make his heir, he seldom mentioned the matter without speaking of you either shortly before or shortly after doing so."

"But what I did for him was so little," I objected.

"He never once mentioned that occurrence," I was promptly snubbed. "What he generally said of you was that you looked like a steady-going young fellow that would keep what you got, instead of running about, boozing and wenching, until you had spent it all. I gathered that he took you for a person a good deal like himself."

"God forbid!" I cried, as again the lawyer leered at me with his dried-up pickle of a face.

"But that isn't all," he went on. "The old man wasn't quite so clever as he thought he was. When he wrote in that name it happened that he laid the will on top of a piece of foolscap which had been left on that desk. He wrote with a steel pen — always used one; quills wore out too fast, he said — and his writing traced the name on the foolscap underneath. Rogers found it there later. Very little escapes that prim little old brown clerk of mine. And the name, Mr. Robert Farrier, was yours."

At once my hopes flew skyward again, carrying every faculty of rational thought with them. I hardly heard him as he went on, except in disjointed phrases: a hundred thousand dollars — accumulation of a lifetime of fortunate speculation — mortgages on real estate chiefly about Philadelphia and Boston, but anywhere far enough away to keep the tax gatherer from hearing of them — never any money in the banks, and none in the lawyer's strong boxes, except for a day or two at a time — the will itself — and with that my hopes dived like a shot duck. Resisting the lawyer's every argument, every offer of stout wrappings, seals and strong box, old Peter had insisted on having the will in his own keeping.

"You will find it right enough when you need it," he had kept reiterating stubbornly when Squire Killian had dwelt upon the way such things have of getting lost. "It shall never be out of my hand's reach, wherever I am, day or night."

"That sounds like the pocket of his old green coat," I hazarded. "He was never seen out of it."

"Or the lining more likely," Killian agreed. "But where is that coat? Have you seen or heard of it since his death?"

"It must be in the house," said I.

"My closest search failed to discover it. The coroner didn't know where it was, and didn't seem to care."

"He had it on the afternoon before he was killed. I remember it distinctly. Did you find any of the clothes he wore that day?" I asked on a sudden thought, and I told him how the rector had raised the question of the old man's clothes the evening before.

"So the dominie thought of that, did he?" he commented sourly. "Well, I found all the rest, where he had left them on the broken chair beside his bed, but not a thread of the coat, though I looked high and low from noon till dark."

"I suppose the old man might have put it on over his nightshirt, and somebody might have stolen it off his dead body before the coroner and the constables got there."

"Not likely. I was there about as soon as anybody, and there was so much blood about that they couldn't have got the coat off him without leaving traces of doing it. Of course, anyone who knew about the will and had a motive for destroying it — and had guessed about its hiding place as you and I have done — might have slipped in and stolen the coat from off the chair before the coroner arrived." But the lawyer's quizzical glance made its eloquent comment on this elaborate hypothesis. "If there was any way in which Rogers could benefit by such an action we might suspect him for want of anyone better. But there isn't," he concluded. "A tramp wouldn't have touched it after seeing that thing on the steps — wouldn't even have walked past that to enter the house. And nobody else would want it."

VI. – OLD PETER WALKS, THEY SAY

Who will benefit, if the will isn't found?" I asked after Killian had let me puzzle over the matter in silence for a minute or two. He shrugged his shoulders.

"Nobody. The state will get it. And the old man hated the state — some trouble with the Crown about usury away back before my time. It was that which caused him to make a will at all, I suspect. He hadn't the ghost of a relative, he assured me."

"Then there is nobody who could have a motive for destroying the will?"

"Nobody — even supposing anybody knew there was a will, except old Sammy and me. I'd swear to that in court."

"But somebody might have thought the coat contained papers which would give a clue as to where the old man had hidden his money — somebody who slipped into the house while the laborer was off to fetch the coroner. Where is the money, the bulk of it, I mean?"

He tossed his bony hands in the air with a gesture singularly out of keeping with his cut-and-dried appearance.

"If I only knew! But aside from a few hundred dollars in my strong box, which happened to be paid in on a fore-closure three days ago, I know no more of its whereabouts than you do."

"Excepting, I suppose, what's out on mortgage and the like," I appended hopefully.

"There's none out on mortgage now — none out at all, in fact. For the past two years old Peter has been turning everything into money — hard money, you understand. No bank credits or notes for him! We were in for bad times, very bad times, he said, when a dollar in gold or silver would be worth ten on the books of a bank. And, God knows, the way things have been going all summer seems to show that he was right. Why, I've known him to sacrifice thirty percent for hard cash."

"You mean that there's actually ninety-eight thousand dollars in gold and silver coin somewhere about that house?" I demanded, resisting the impulse to cram my hat on my head and start running up the hill.

"Well," he grinned at me. "I know that in the past two years I've paid him approximately that amount across his table in the dead of night, taking one occasion with another; and none of it has gone out through my hands."

"But in that case," I cried, sick with apprehension, "what's to prevent anybody from finding the money and walking off with it?"

"To begin with, it must be pretty well hidden, or I should have found it yesterday. Also, have you considered the weight and bulk of such a sum in specie? If it were all in golden guineas, there would be twenty thousand of them, nearly. But there was a large amount of silver; and the gold itself was of all sorts, Friedrichs, Louis, Pauls, Greek byzants, Arabian dinars, mohurs from Hindustan — coins that haven't seen daylight since some of our first families were silent partners of the Madagascar pirates."

"But a man with all night to work in," I was beginning.

"Tush, tush!" he interrupted impatiently. Nobody has a key, but me and the new tenant, the Frenchman; and the place has not been tampered with. I went up again early this morning to make sure."

Forgetful of the rules of courtesy in my excitement, I sprang to my feet.

"I would like to go up there now," I said. "The search may be a long one; and when Monsieur de Saint Loup takes possession, it will have to cease. Will you — have you the time to come with me at once?"

"To what end?" he asked with irritating calmness.

"To the end that persons breaking in shall not find the money and make away with it," I answered hotly.

"They'll not. If any such could find it, I should have found it when I searched the place for the coat. I did find his more accessible hiding places and, my impetuous young friend, they were both — empty."

"Empty?"

"Empty. And, by the dust in them, they hadn't been used for weeks. I left them open, by the way, so that any chance prowler would see them and decide that he had come too late."

"Then, you don't think — "

"No. I'm morally certain the money is still in the house or on the place, and so well hidden that we need have no fear of the wrong people finding it."

"But in that case — " I moved toward the door.

"You want to begin tearing the house down? Well, you cannot. Until that will is found, remember, you have no more right in the matter than anybody at all. Find me the will, find me that old green coat, and I'll wager all I'm worth that you can do as you like. Why, my boy," he went on kindly, "should we find the money now, I should probably be compelled to turn it over to the state; and then, even if the will turned up later — Well, I don't suppose you have ever tried to recover any property after the state had got its hands on it, have you?"

He took his departure shortly after that, and I went along with him as far as the counting-house, as completely tantalized a man as there was in America that morning. Already I had begun to plan a search for that old redingote. But it was going to be hard to find. If anybody living in the neighborhood had taken it, it was too well known, too sure to be recognized, for him to risk wearing it, though he had no other coat to his back. When he found that its pockets contained nothing to his purpose, he would hide it, bury it — or burn it.

At the thought of the only proof of my inheritance being

37

wiped out in such a manner my body broke into a perspiration in spite of the frosty air of the morning. But the alternative was no more cheering. Had the thief been some prowling tramp, with more courage than the lawyer was willing to think possible, he might have sold it at the next town up or down the river, or he might have kept it to wear as soon as he was far enough away to feel safe from the chance of its being recognized. In that case it was now probably moving farther and farther away from me with every moment. Already it might be in Albany, whence roads branched out in every direction; or, if its wearer had managed to stow away on some barge or sloop, it might even now be lost for ever in the slums of New York. But at least I could inspect the old-clothes shops in the neighboring towns. So I hurried through the counting-room and into my uncle's private room with the intention of asking for a two days' holiday.

It turned out that I did not have to make my request, which was as well, for I found him in no mood for granting favors, or indeed for listening to me at all. A letter which must have reached him through some private agency — the post was not due until the morrow — lay open on his table before him; and it was evident that he was maintaining only with difficulty the air of unruffled calm which he cultivated as appropriate to his resemblance to the Father of Our Country.

"I am glad that you have put in an appearance at last, Robert," he began at once with a glance at the banjo clock that ticked so deliberately on the wall behind his left shoulder. "I wish to take horse instanter for a trip among our customers. They have become intolerably lax in the matter of remittances. You are to bring back with you as large a portion as possible of what may be overdue. A list of them and their delinquencies will be handed you in the counting-room. Return to your house at once now and pack your saddle-bags for a trip of a fortnight. Pray make haste. I desire you to be off within the hour."

By bringing it in as an excuse for my tardiness I might have told him of Squire Killian's call and his amazing news, but I had never seen him so disturbed and I forbore. After all, what I could have told him was so indefinite, and the course of action which I had proposed for myself, and which I could now carry out without neglecting his affairs, partook so much of the nature of a forlorn hope that to impose it on his patience at that moment seemed like an impertinence. But there was another to whom I was determined to tell it, however it might interfere with my uncle's wishes for my immediate departure. Moreover, it seemed to me to be a physical impossibility to leave town without apologizing to

38

Felicity for my contemptible behavior of the night before. The thought of spending the next two weeks without knowing that I had her forgiveness and absolution was more than I could bear.

So, with pistols in my holsters, packed saddlebags and greatcoat strapped to the cantle, I drew rein at my uncle's door a little less than an hour later in the strong sunshine of the brilliant autumn morning. The prospect of my inheritance, uncertain though it was, enlivened all my thoughts. Was I not riding out to establish it? But only the Haytian waiting-woman came down the stairs in response to the message I had sent up by Barry to the effect that as I was leaving town for a fortnight I desired a few words with Miss Paige.

"Miss F'lic'ty have gone out to walk with that French gentleman, with that M'sou de Saint Loup, Mr. Farrier, sir," she informed me, and added with ready sympathy at sight of the disappointment which I could not help showing, "She will be very disappointed that she missed you."

"Do you really think she will be disappointed, Vashti, or are you only trying to cheer me up?" I asked, smiling.

"She surely will be, Mr. Farrier, sir. She'll be angry, too, that all that made her miss you was a walk with that French gentleman."

"Is that true?" I cried with a lover's delight.

"Of course, it's true. Why would she care to walk with a little fat Frenchman when she could be talking with a young gentleman of her own age and quality?"

"Vashti," I laughed, "there's a dollar for you."

But to my surprise she absolutely refused to take the coin I proffered. I would not believe what she said if she took money for it, she insisted gravely.

"But I wish you would let me ask you one question, Mr. Farrier, sir," she went on seriously. "I wish to ask you, do you know if that French gentleman has ever been to Hayti?"

"Is that why you stared at him so hard that first afternoon on the road?" I asked.

"Well, sir, I wondered if it was the reason why he stared so hard at me: if he had been in Hayti maybe, and I reminded him of something."

"I don't know, Vashti," I said, and again I offered payment for the happiness she had given me, only to be again refused. I swung into the saddle and tightened the reins; but she continued to stand, looking up at me with large dark eyes so filled with a wistful friendliness that I added impulsively, "I wish you would give your mistress a message for me, Vashti. I wish you would tell her that I called to ask her pardon before I left."

39

"Yes, sir, Mr. Farrier, I'll surely tell her that, sir. But you got her pardon before you ask it."

"I have?" I exclaimed, incredulous.

"Yes, sir. She told me last night when I putting her to bed. She say you felt terrible. And then she laugh and say she don't feel terrible at all."

She spoke so seriously, there was so complete an absence of the time-serving lady's maid's vicarious coquetry from her grave mouth and solemn eyes, that I could not have disbelieved her, had I wished to do so.

"God bless you, Vashti," I cried, and rode away in such a golden mist of joy that the steeple of Lithgow church was shining across the river opposite me before I thought again of my uncle's affairs or even of Squire Killian's strange story. Then I began to scan each wayfarer and the loungers beneath the trees at every village tavern door for a glimpse of a worn green coat. In every town I went from the stores where I transacted my uncle's business to the pawnshops and old clothes dealers, but without success. And everywhere I heard the same story of deplorable conditions.

At a crossroads about five miles out of the town a new broad-sheet, tacked to a tree and headed, "Wolf — $100.00 — Reward," made me pull up to read it, and I saw my uncle's name among the signers. It stated that the town council of New Dortrecht offered this sum for the head of the timber wolf which had committed the outrages set forth below. Followed a brief account of the slaying of Armitage and Mr. Sackville's Nero, and of the pursuit of the clergyman himself, also of an atrocity committed since my departure. Old Sammy Rogers, Squire Killian's clerk, had been found dead, his throat torn open, on almost the same spot where Armitage had been killed two weeks before.

My thoughts grew busy with the possible implications of this news, as I rode onward. What could old Sammy have been about in the miser's garden? He had known about the will and, with his opportunities of knowing everything that concerned his employer's clients, he must have been aware of those numerous and large remittances of money and where they went. I called to mind everything that I could remember about him: the fat, solemn little man in his neat drab clothes, precise and punctual as the town hall clock, without an interest in life, one would have said, beyond the copying of briefs and the drawing of conveyances. Was it possible that the thought of those thousands of dollars hidden away had lured even him to his death?

As I trotted through the High Street, I had to struggle against the desire to stop at the lawyer's office and learn the details of this affair instead of pressing on to my uncle's counting-house at once in order to get the money I had collected into his safe before the place was closed for the night. It happened, however, that the lawyer from his window chanced to see me coming and ran out bareheaded into the street to stop me.

"You've seen the notices, doubtless. Yes. Poor Sammy!" He cut short the rather perfunctory expressions of regret which I had begun. "Who'd have thought a fat, drab little old moth like him would have blundered into that candle flame? Meant to do you a good turn. That's what we've got to think. Had an idea too, evidently. Hammer and chisel beside him when they found him, but I can't find a sign that he had used them anywhere, though he must have been out all that night. It rained all that night, and he was soaking wet. Well, this isn't what I stopped you for. It's that green redingote I want to speak of."

"You mean, you've found it?"

"I think I know where we can get our hands on it. Can you meet me here at my office at ten tonight — with your pistols?" And he brought his hand down on my near holster with a smack that made my horse start forward, weary though the creature was.

"Armitage's place is haunted, it seems," he went on, screwing up his mouth into an expression of preternatural gravity. "Old Peter walks, they say, or has the last two nights. Been seen by three witnesses credible in their own conceit, green coat and all quite perfect, with a lantern in his hand and a ghastly green light all round him. Are you game to go and help me lay this poor wandering spirit?"

"I'll be here," I said stoutly, although at this distance I will admit that I don't know whether it was the near prospect of the fulfillment of my hopes or superstitious fear that sent a thrill up my spine.

"Be on your guard as you come," he cautioned me.

"You mean that the wolf has been down in the streets again?" I asked.

"Oh, to be sure," he replied ironically; "and for one who has actually seen it a dozen have been chased to their doors by it. The council has had to bolster up the morale of the watch." He nodded in the direction of the town hall across the way with grim jocularity. The narrow street was already thick with the early twilight, but I could make out the two constables going on duty and observed that in addition to their halberts and lanterns each had a short blunderbuss slung across his left shoulder.

"It's against them I meant to warn you," the lawyer

explained. "They are in a state to loose off at a mouse. So sing out promptly if you are challenged."

VII. – DE RETZ

Either my fortnight's absence had given me the power to see my uncle more clearly or the accumulating anxieties of business had told upon him to a remarkable degree since my departure. I was shocked at the change in him the moment I entered his private office. His face was pale and deeply lined, his eyes dim and swollen as from the lack of sleep. The old air of lofty equanimity, which with youthful intolerance I had put down as no more than pompousness, was gone altogether. He snatched up the list of customers which I laid down before him along with the bag of money, and his glance went straight to the footings at the bottom of it.

"This means that you have brought this sum in cash?" he demanded, although I had totaled the cash and notes separately and marked each of them clearly for what it was. "If so the house can go on, at least for the present," he added.

If it had not been pathetic, it might have been amusing to observe how he gradually regained something of his customary manner after I had assured him on that score.

"My sending you out at all on such an errand doubtless apprised you in some measure of our present situation, Robert," he went on. "I do not know that Barclay and Barclay have ever been constrained to take such a course before. But the credit of the strongest houses is impaired by the prevailing stringency, and I should be less than candid with you if I did not add that I have been and am increasingly embarrassed, if only for the time being."

One saw that he credited himself with extraordinary magnanimity for admitting that a business controlled by him could be embarrassed even in a period of national business adversity. By the time I had finished my oral comments on my report he had talked himself into a fair imitation of his usual self-confidence and self-esteem. He cut short my apologies for not having been a more successful agent and asked me to come home to supper with him with precisely his old assumption of benignity.

"Felicity will be delighted to see you," he went on, thus making her also a beneficiary. "I fear it has been dull for her since Monsieur de Saint Loup's departure last week. They appeared to find each other mutually entertaining."

"Indeed?" said I, and had food for thought to last me to my uncle's door. I could not but be struck however with the changed appearance of the streets as we passed along. Although the early nightfall was already complete, it was not yet half-past six, and ordinarily the footways should have been lively with the final activities of closing time. But tonight the rare lamps swung above empty streets and shone on closed shop-fronts. At the tobacconist's the last shutters were going up with nervous haste; and the door of Dirk Brinker's dramshop, which had stood open until eleven o'clock, winter and summer, since I could remember, showed no more than a ruddy light through the barred peephole in its upper panel. Three or four passers-by, evidently belated, scuttled along at a gait more appropriate to a winter night than to a crisp autumn evening.

It was like my Uncle Barclay to take these signs of the general panic as an affront to himself in his capacity of town councilor. From them he turned his glance upon me and saw the butts of my pistols projecting from my greatcoat pockets where I had thrust them when I dismounted.

"You have already caught the prevailing hysteria, I observe," he remarked. Had it not been for his tone, I suppose I might have told him why I carried them, of Squire Killian's project for the night, about the missing green coat, the miser's will and how my future seemed to be wrapped up in the mystery. But that drily contemptuous note of his always shut me up. I had made up my mind that the whole thing was still too nebulous to arouse in him anything more than an amused or slightly impatient skepticism. Anything unusual or inherently unlikely effected him that way. So I replied merely that I had not wished to send them to the stable on my saddle, loaded as they were.

"By the way," he went on, "Monsieur de Saint Loup's wolfhound arrived the other day. I never saw a more magnificent animal. If this monster troubles us again, I mean to put him on its trail. Had the hound not been so newly arrived, I should have tried it the morning after Rogers was slain. But he is so powerful and looked so savage that I doubted our ability to control him until he knew us better. He has a surly way with strangers, though your cousin has won his confidence."

I was given a demonstration of this the moment we entered the house. Felicity was standing in the hall with her hand on the broad brass-studded collar of a huge wolfish beast that strained toward us, growling, the hair upon its neck erect, its long fangs exposed.

"Down, De Retz, down," she chided, and the hound ceased at once to pull against her hand, though it continued to growl softly. "Good evening, Cousin Robert. Welcome home. Come and make friends with this bellicose French gentleman."

I have been familiar with dogs all my life. So when I had

43

followed her into the drawing-room I went up to the animal without any fear, although without any of the liking one instinctively feels for a fine creature. Larger than the Irish wolfhound, it bore a closer resemblance to its traditional enemy than any other wolfhound I had ever seen. Its color would prove to be the very gray of the twilight, were it out of doors, I guessed. Its eyes were extraordinary in their look of ferocity mingled with intelligence; and their gaze met mine and met it steadily as long as I looked at them, instead of turning aside after a second or so, as an ordinary dog's will do.

"Shake hands, De Retz. Give Cousin Robert your paw like the great gentleman you are. Friends of mine must be friends of each other. Isn't it delightful how quickly he has picked up English, Robert? I had to speak French entirely to him when he came," she ran on, as the hound grudgingly extended one huge paw and permitted me to take it in my hand.

"That's a good dog, a really great gentleman, Monsieur le Cardinal," she commended; whereupon the great brute reared on its hind legs, fore paws on her slight shoulders, its head on a level with her face, red tongue lolling, eyes rolling with delight.

One sees such a thing done often enough by an affectionate animal. To this day I do not know why it should have disgusted and infuriated me as it did, unless I had some faint and unrealized adumbration of what was to come. Or it may have been no more than the red glare in the beast's eyes as they caught the fire-light. Something, at all events, in that tableau of the beautiful girl with her bare neck and lovely arms in the embrace of that fawning animal revolted me.

"Get down! Down, you damned brute!" I shouted, and made a stride toward him, my clenched hand lifted. He dropped instantly, but snarling and showing his teeth.

"Robert, take care! Quiet, De Retz, quiet. What possessed you, Robert? I was in no danger. He adores me. He thought you meant to strike me probably."

"Then he was very much mistaken," I retorted grimly.

"But he wouldn't hurt me for worlds. However, I don't think our uncle cares particularly for his presence even yet. So we'll continue your acquaintance with him some afternoon on a walk." And she arose from her knees beside the hound, which she had been pacifying with caresses while she spoke, and rang for Barry to lead the creature away to the stable for the night.

"It's a lucky thing for Monsieur de Saint Loup that his hound didn't arrive in town before this mysterious wolf began its ravages," I said when we were alone again. "He looks so capable of any deviltry that nobody would ever have believed him innocent."

"Oh, but you saw the very worst side of him," she took me up warmly. "He is horrid to people who are afraid of him or —"

"Afraid?" I scoffed.

"Or those he feels don't like him, I was about to say. Henry, my coachman, hates him, fears and loathes him, calls him a wolf in dog's clothing, and threatens to refuse to go on sleeping in the stable if De Retz continues to be kept there. The horses gave trouble the first evening unfortunately, and Henry's imagination has been running riot ever since. Since Vashti has been brewing a charm, I suspect."

"Brewing a charm?"

"Yes. You don't know the Haytians, do you? Vashti, you must understand it, is what they call a conjure-woman. Her Haytian origin greatly enhances her reputation for that kind of thing, of course. And I am always catching her at mixing up queer messes or tying dreadful little odds and ends together."

Unpleasant as the incident had been, at least it had carried us over the awkwardness of our first meeting since my abominable outbreak two weeks before.

"Vashti had a message to give to you from me," I said. "Did she deliver it, Felicity?"

"She did, Robert. And I understand that she gave you my answer to it at once. That is the trouble with having a maid who has been one's nurse since one was a baby. One tells her things no lady should ever tell her maid. I meant to leave you in sackcloth and ashes for days."

"How did you know I was in sackcloth and ashes?" I challenged in answer to the smile that lurked behind the mock annoyance in her eyes.

"Because I knew you were a gentleman — Cousin," she tossed at me.

"Very well, but be it understood, I don't retract my words, however much I deplore what I did," I asserted.

"The words were as mad as all the rest," she told me with an airy scorn; and just then our uncle entered to inform us that supper was served.

The meal and his customary single glass of port appeared to complete the restoration of his spirits. He opened a vein of banter so stately as to amount to elephantine archness, begging Felicity, if she had any "private intelligence" of the probable date of Monsieur de Saint Loup's return, to let him know it, and retailing to me the circumstances of the Frenchman's delayed departure and his own shrewd surmises about the reason for it.

"How he could have decided about the alterations and furnishing of his house if your cousin had not been here, I do

45

not know, for he called upon her for her advice three times in every day," he informed me.

I didn't like this fooling. For while his eyes shone with mischievousness there was a satisfied smirk about his mouth, as if Saint Loup's attentions to his niece pleased as well as flattered him. This I guessed that she also was well aware of; but she turned it deftly and by quoting a few of the Frenchman's more high-flown compliments quieted my jealous fears at the same time. She made me tell her of my journey, and played and sang for us as on our first evening together, so that, eager though I was to investigate the strange doings at Armitage's, it was with keen regret that I made my plea of fatigue a little before ten and set out for the lawyer's office. My uncle would have rung for Barry to let me out. But with those warm Southern manners of hers she insisted on herself going to the door with me, and I felt truly now that I was forgiven.

"Will you not look to your priming?" she asked at sight of the pistols in my greatcoat pockets, and added, "Cousin" with the ghost of a smile.

For answer I took her hand and kissed it with an exaggeration of Monsieur de Saint Loup's courtliness but with a careful avoidance of anything approaching his fervor.

I found Squire Killian with a long well-oiled rifle lying across the desk in front of him and a title-abstract of many yellow pages in his hands. He did not speak but gave me his customary sour nod, rose and reached for his greatcoat that hung on the peg behind him.

"Squire," I said, for I had had my first opportunity to do a little thinking about the matter as I walked from my uncle's, "what motive would anybody have to spend his nights masquerading round old Peter's garden? It must be a chilly sort of pastime this frosty weather."

"Meaning you've a suspicion it's actually the old man's restless ghost, and you want to back out?" he gibed.

"Meaning nothing of the sort," I retorted indignantly. "But why — "

"Because it's a convenient way for somebody to go round up there, hunting for the money, and has the added advantage of scaring off everybody else."

"He has good courage, whoever he is, to go on after what happened to Sammy Rogers. Look here," I cried, struck by a sudden thought, "isn't it possible that Sammy is responsible for the whole business, took the coat and did the haunting? He knew about the will and the money as nobody else did. These later stories of the ghost may be simply the result of earlier ones which had a real foundation."

"No," Killian replied. "It won't hold water. What would Sammy have been doing up there that first morning before the coroner got there, which is when the coat disappeared. Also, nobody heard of a ghost until after Sammy was killed."

"Come on, then," I exclaimed impatiently. "We'll get him, dead or alive, if he walks tonight."

"Ah, but there we must be careful," he warned. "A man isn't outlawed for playing ghost, you know. We cannot fire at him. These weapons are in case the wolf should be on the prowl again. Don't allow yourself to forget that for a moment."

He blew out the candles; we slipped into the street and set off up the hill by a circuitous route as quietly as possible, lest the unknown haunter see us and so be put upon his guard. We had, moreover, no wish to come within range of the nervous blunderbusses of the watch. Indeed the lawyer led me to the far side of Gallows Hill before coming out upon the road. He crossed this and, with a readiness that showed how thoroughly he must have examined the ground by daylight, plunged into a narrow wood path which circled round until by the slope under my feet I realized that we were descending through the hanging grove behind old Peter's house and must presently come out into his back garden. Stars began to shine between the tops of the pine trees; I made out the silhouette of a low roof and chimneys against the sky; in front of me the lawyer halted; and putting out my hand I felt the rough stones of one side of the breach in the garden wall.

"We'll find a spot somewhere to your left," he whispered, "where you can cover the south and west walls of the house. I'll do the same to the northeast, covering the front gate as you will cover this gap. There are no other means of access or egress. If you start the quarry, cut him off from this gap and yell, 'North' or 'East,' according to the way he starts running. In like circumstances I'll shout 'West' or 'South.' You understand?"

I told him that I did but thought I could better the plan, and I suggested that instead of rushing the ghost on sight we observe his movements and so possibly save ourselves trouble in any search we might wish to make later. Only when he seemed about to leave the enclosure need we pound upon him.

To all this Squire Killian gave his entire approval. But he made it a point to keep with me until I had chosen my place of observation and, once gone, startled me by stealing back to advise a position with the garden wall close behind me.

"This infernal wolf," he whispered. "No use giving him the chance to get you as he did the rector's Nero." And off he crept again, leaving me with the last thought I would have chosen to entertain in those surroundings.

The garden was full of strong starlight; and although the house in front and the wood behind me were masses of impenetrable shadow, nothing of the bigness of man or wolf could have moved unseen alongs its neglected pathways. But anyone who has lain out in the forest at night above some salt-lick, waiting with every sense alert for the first sound of the approach of the great wild creature which is presently to be aimed at by the starshine along a rifle barrel, may form some notion of my state of mind. Let him add to that, however, the thought of the human game we hunted, the sum of money at stake, and what it meant to me, the hazard of that diabolical wolf, and the grisly associations of the spot, if he would do me justice on my later conduct. For it is one thing to be a rationalist in the sunshine of broad noon and quite another to dismiss the superstitious terrors which steal upon the mind in midnight darkness.

A score of yards from the dilapidated cold-frame in which I crouched the ground was hardly dry of the blood of two abominable killings whose bestial perpetrator was still at large. People whom I knew believed they had seen the unquiet spirit of one of the victims walking this very ground, some of them as lately as twenty-four hours ago. The enclosure and the wood behind it were full of noises, little mysterious rustlings, the crack of a twig, an eery pattering on the dry and matted leaves. An owl hooted; and my hands flew of their own volition, it seemed to me, to the butts of the pistols which I had drawn from my pockets and laid ready on the rotting board in front of me. At the solemn tolling of midnight by the clock in the town below, my memory echoed with those funeral cadences spoken on the platform of the Castle of Elsinore.

Also I was growing uncomfortably cold, stiff and cramped, so that I found in my heart to wish even for the appearance of the great wolf to give a term to his intolerable vigil. As I shifted my aching body, I glimpsed above the wall to my right front the crown of Gallows Hill. Like a gallows itself rose between me and the house the two uprights and cross-beam above old Peter's well. From it the counter weight to the bucket hung aslant like the head of a suspended body which was lost in the shadows below. But if the sight changed their subject it wrought little betterment in my thoughts — that smooth, round-topped eminence bare of tree and bush as if blasted by a curse, and the stark frame so close and so like the grim one which once had crowned the hill.

Stay! Had something moved within the range of my strained vision? Was that a sound, other than the noises of the

48

night, and from the direction of the house? I racked my memory for another sound like the dry click of a falling wooden latch, my eyes the while probing the dark mass of the house till they ached with the effort. At once the weakness of our arrangements became apparent to me. We had made no provision in case our quarry should have been beforehand with us and already lurking in the shadows close to the house when we arrived. That he might have means of access to the house itself had never crossed our minds. Out of sight of each other, we had devised no means of communication; an attempt by either of us to approach the other, if made with sufficient caution to avoid betraying our presence, might cause the one who made it to be mistaken by the other either for the man we sought or for the wolf.

Yet now the sound came again, unmistakably that of a latch when I had my attention fixed upon it. The door at the top of those stone steps so lately and twice over stained with human blood had opened and closed. Those sounds could mean nothing else. But did they mean that someone had come out or gone in? To my mortification I perceived that in the depths of the shadows round the house it had been possible for someone either to approach the door or at that very moment to be leaving it without my being able to see him from where I crouched. In either case there appeared to be but one course for me to take. For if I dashed forward and he were inside, he must stay there or else rush through the front door into the arms of Killian; and if he had come out, my charge would drive him round the house and things would work out as we had planned them.

A pistol in each hand, I sprang forward with a shout. By the stone steps a shadow only less dark than the rest whirled and leapt at me. But my foot had struck the corner of a half-buried brick in the garden border, and I went headlong. There was a snarl and the snap of jaws in my ears, the reek of bestial hide in my nostrils. A great, hairy bulk shot over me in a leap that would have reached my throat, had I not been falling. The darkness was split with the blast and flame of Killian's rifle so close that I felt its heat upon my cheek. Then he had wrenched the pistols out of my hands and was kneeling above me, peering now right, now left, now over his shoulders into the shadows, the muzzles of the weapons darting in each direction with his glance.

VIII. — THE CRUSOE TOUCH

"Are you hurt?" he whispered after several moments of silence broken only by quick-drawn breaths. "Did he gash you in passing? If ever I saw a lucky stumble, that of yours — "

"If it hadn't been for your shot — How did you happen to be at hand?"

"What made you charge like that?" he countered. We had risen to our feet and, having given me back my pistols, he began mechanically to reload his rifle.

"I thought I heard somebody enter or leave the house. I could have sworn I heard the latch fall twice," I began apologetically. "I couldn't see and like a fool — "

"And I could have sworn somebody was inside the house," he interrupted me. "I saw the light move twice in the front room. As I crept forward to peep through the window it moved toward the back and went out. So I slipped round here to see if it reappeared in the kitchen window. My son, I'm glad I did. Now," he added briskly, snapping down the battery on the freshly primed pan of his weapon, "let us go in and try to find out what we did see and hear. Our bird will have flown for the night after this — if he was ever here. So there's no need of caution against him.

"Door locked," he went on, when we had mounted the little porch. He produced a key and flung the door wide, letting out a breath of the stuffiness of closed houses. "Now for a light."

I do not know what I expected to see that held me so tense while the flint flashed and the glowing tinder was nursed until at last a candle flamed. At what it revealed when we passed through the kitchen into the large front room I started, though this was no more than piled-up chairs and tables in crates and carpets and rugs in sacking. I remembered at once that I had been told that Monsieur de Saint Loup's furniture had come in the sloop which brought his great hound. Evidently the stuff had been brought up here and left to await his arrival. Meanwhile the lawyer moved about the room, stooping and holding the candle now on this side, now on that, so that its light fell strongly on the bare boards of the floor.

"No tallow droppings," he grumbled to himself. "So much for that light I thought I saw — and yet — if there was more dust to show foot-tracks, I'd be better satisfied."

"Quick — the candle! Look here!" I burst out.

Wandering rather aimlessly, I had approached the fireplace and at his mention of the floor I had looked down at the coating of fine ashes which had sifted out upon the broad smooth hearthstone. In this, clear and sharp as if it were not five minutes old, was the imprint of a naked human foot. The lawyer was beside me in one long stride, bending so close that his lank hair brushed my cheek.

"Well, Mr. Robinson Crusoe," he said at length, "has our wolf grown human feet, or what?"

He set the candle on the floor, and as if by tacit consent we knelt to examine the impression with lips tight shut lest an unguarded breath disturb the light ash that preserved each outline and contour. So we remained for perhaps a minute. Then Squire Killian threw his weight back upon his heels and leapt upright with astonishing agility for a man of his dried-up and stiffened appearance.

"One of your pistols — quick," he demanded in a whisper. "Whoever made that must still be in the house."

"Or slipped out while we've been in here."

"Couldn't. I locked the back door behind us."

"The front door." I meant that the intruder might have left by that while we were entering at the back.

"Bolted on the inside." He waved the candle at it. "I marked that the moment we came in here. By George, we've got him now. I'll go ahead. You keep at my right shoulder, holding the candle high in your left hand, your pistol in your right in case he tries any monkey-tricks. This room first." And he flung wide the doors of an elaborate system of cupboards flanking the chimney, the only possible hiding place in the long bare room. The three bedrooms opening out of this came next, then the kitchen. That was all. And in not one of them did we find a trace of anybody. Every window was fast nailed down. Every door had a lock and a key which we were careful to turn behind us. So there was no possibility that our man had treated us to a game of puss-in-the-corner. Not only was he not in the house, but it seemed clear that nobody could have been in it since we entered. Yet had he left just before that, he must have been standing within a yard or two of the wolf when the brute sprang at me. In that case my rush might well have saved his life.

Back beside the hearth again Killian pulled up the only chair and dropped into it, his elbows on his knees, his chin in his cupped hands, staring down at the foot-print by the light of the candle which I held above it.

"We have our choice of two explanations," he said at length, and added with his sour grin, "Both of them are impossible."

"What are they?"

"Well, the one," he began, taking a twist of tobacco from his pocket and shaving off a morsel which with a motion incredibly swift and surreptitious he slipped between his cheek and gums, "is that our friend here" — he pointed his remark with a jet of saliva that just missed the footprint — "had the audacity to slip out and away at the moment when the attack of the wolf had left us in disorder. If he were already on the porch with the door locked behind him, that is just possible, I suppose."

"I don't believe it," said I. "The wolf was on the porch — at least on the steps — must have been by the way it sprang at me. What's the alternative?"

"Only that I was wrong in thinking I saw a light, that you only imagined you heard the latch, and that the man who made that had departed before we arrived in the garden at all."

"And went round barefoot because he liked the feeling of the cold boards on his naked soles?" I gibed. "No, sir, he was here, heard us, and slipped off his shoes so that we shouldn't hear him."

"But why take off his stockings too?"

"I give it up," I began, and stopped with a nervous laugh, for the thought which had just struck me made me shiver. "Look here, Squire. Did they lay out old Peter in this room? Well, supposing they did, they might have — not stood him up exactly — but so handled him that one of his feet made that imprint."

"Did you ever see old Peter's feet, notice them at the inquest?" he demanded. "To say nothing of the freshness of that track there. Look at it." Already some imperceptible draft had begun to blur its edges. "Besides, I've been over this house four times, examining everything. That hearth, for instance, I sounded all over, thinking there might be a cavity under it."

"The truckmen who brought the furniture," I persisted. "One of them might have been barefoot if it was a warm day."

"A truckman with a foot like that! Look at the delicacy of it, the high arch, the narrow heel. It might almost be a woman's. By George," he cried, dropping to his knees and taking the candle from my hand, "we don't know that it wasn't. Here, have a fresh look at it. You're more of an age to judge of a wench's naked foot than I am."

"It looks like the foot of an aristocrat at all events. Monsieur de Saint Loup might have made it, if he hadn't been in New York for the past week."

"Certainly no common tramp could make it, no humble scalawag from hereabouts either." The lawyer was judicial again. "But the spook himself has always been fully dressed, by all accounts."

I stood up, stretching my arms and yawning elaborately.

" 'T is certain he'll not come back while we sit here — probably not tonight, after the close shave we have given him. And I am beginning to remember that I was up and in the saddle before sunrise."

The honest truth was that I had lost all consciousness of fatigue in the excitement of the last two hours. But my nerves
52

were twitching with a tension that seemed to fill that room. To my overstrained senses the place was a-crawl with stealthy movements which I only just failed to catch out of the corners of my eyes. To remain there another moment while the lawyer frowned in silence over that mysterious mark became intolerable.

"This butters no parsnips!" I exclaimed. "I'm for bed."

He gave a stubborn shake of the head, but rose, nevertheless.

"One good carte de visite deserves another," he chuckled and sent a final jet of tobacco juice fairly into the center of the footprint. "If the rascal returns, at least he'll see that we've not missed his tracks." He glanced at his watch, snapping the heavy silver case when he had done so. "Nearly three in the morning. For two farthings I'd start on a wolf-hunt this minute, if I knew where I could get hold of a good hound at this ungodly hour."

I was about to let this pass with a merely perfunctory reply, when a sudden thought struck me. I was, as I have said, unaware of any fatigue; sleep seemed out of the question; and if we should go to my uncle's and could wake Henry, Felicity's coachman, without arousing the people in the house, I thought we might borrow De Retz for the hunt, provided Squire Killian really wished to do so. He assented eagerly upon my describing the animal to him, but he checked me with a low hiss of caution when I was for bolting through the garden ahead of him in my haste to put the business in hand.

" 'T would be just like this cunning beast to lie in wait for us," he whispered. So we moved into the road with circumspection and scouted each turning and dooryard hedge although, after the creepy garden and the haunted air of the little house, the streets with their walks of brick and flags and their prosaic hitching-posts, quiet and substantial in the clear starlight, looked singularly reassuring. There was no sound but the beat of our footsteps. The dogs were silent. The windows of my uncle's house were as blank as all the rest. But, as we stole up the alley that gave access to the stable, I was startled by a dim glow ahead and the round tones of my uncle's voice sharpened by annoyance.

"Sleep on the kitchen floor? Certainly not. Go back to your room in the stable at once, man. I never heard anything so nonsensical."

"Yes, seh, Misteh Barclay. Jes' as you say." It was Henry who spoke, submissive but infinitely stubborn at the same time, as only a trusted servant knows how to be. "Kitchen floor is no place fo' stablehand, and tha's a fac'. I'll jes' sleep down heah on the nice sof' grass rest o' the night. Most

53

mohnin' now anyhow."

"You'll do nothing of the kind, you old idiot," thundered my uncle. "You'd catch your death of it. Back to your room instanter. Do you hear me?"

"Yes, seh, Misteh Barclay, Ah hea's you all right. But Ah don' go back to that stable no mo' to sleep w'ile that wolfhoun' dog stay theah. Ah jus' plum don' do that."

"Why, the hound won't hurt you. He cannot," my uncle cried petulantly. "In that great loosebox with the gate bolted what could he do to you up in your room, man?"

"Ah don' know, seh. That's jus' it. Ah don' know what that wolfhoun' dog can't do. But he don' stay in no loose-box afteh dark, that houn' don't. He don' stay in the stable even. That Ah knows. An' a houn' what can let hisself out o' a loose-box an' out o' a stable too, Ah reckon can do what he please 'foh I can stop him."

Squire Killian and I had been for some moments on the scene of the disturbance by this time; and I know that I at least was at some pains to keep all traces of a natural amusement from showing on my face when the actors in it should finally observe our presence. Remembering what Felicity had told me of the old servant's superstitious fear of the great hound, I could easily guess what had happened. Frightened by some restless movements of the animal, Henry had bolted out and attempted to gain entrance to the house with the unhappy result of waking my uncle.

"Let me take the hound, Uncle Barclay," said I, stepping forward. "That ought to settle this difficulty for the rest of the night at least." And when I had accounted for our presence by telling him no more than that the wolf had been seen in Armitage's garden since midnight, I proceeded to outline Squire Killian's project. I think my uncle would have granted a request far more unreasonable than the loan of another man's dog in order to escape from the horns of the dilemma on which his authority and his dignity were alike impaled. He asked no inconvenient questions, but candle in hand, himself led the way to the stable, though I protested that his health ran some risk from further exposure to the night air. It was Henry who would have stopped me at the door.

"You fixin' to take that wolfhoun' dog out, Misteh Robert? Then you be mighty perspicacious how you approach him. He mighty ferocious with folks he don' know."

"Look here, Henry," my uncle commanded, and as the man hung back, "no. Come in here. Look at this gate. There is no room between the top and the ceiling for the hound to leap over it, even supposing the creature could leap so high; and a

54

man might have trouble to reach between the bars and slide this great bolt. Can't you see that?"

"Yes, seh. Misteh Barclay. Ah see that all right."

"Well, then!"

"Houn's paw go where man's hand can't slip through," Henry had begun, when my uncle burst out:

"You sluggard! Haven't I told you it was absolutely essential that this place be kept clean? What is the meaning of this rubbish?"

He was staring at a little heap of bones, a wad of hair such as some animal might have left by rubbing on the sharp end of a fence-rail, and on top of all, a cock's head, its red comb and bloody neck brilliant in the candle-light.

"Must have ovehlooked that when I swep' out las' evenin', Misteh Barclay."

"Overlooked it in the middle of the runway?"

"Pretty dark heah evenin's, seh."

My uncle snorted.

"There's the beast, Robert." He opened the gate a few inches and thrust the candle inside. "The leash hangs on the wall at your elbow."

I took down the leash and stepped within. Stretched prone, hind legs gathered under him, his head extended on his fore paws, the pupils of his eyes shrunk to pencil-points in the sudden light, the great hound looked formidable enough. But I anticipated no hostility after our introduction of the early evening.

"Come, De Retz," I said briskly and was stooping to snap the leash on to his collar when, without a premonitory movement, without so much as a sound, he flew at me. Had not Squire Killian's interest in the magnificent animal led him to follow me into the loose-box, his rifle still in his hand, those great fangs would have been buried in the arm which I threw up to guard my throat. As it was, a thrust of the rifle butt sent the brute staggering against the wall. The creature whirled upon us, snarling but shaken.

"By God!" I cried, furious with fright and anger. "Hand me that whip from the rack, Uncle Barclay. No. Hand it to me. This fellow needs a lesson."

But my uncle would not.

"Come out, Robert," he commanded, his face quite white. "And you too, Squire. The animal is vicious. He is not ours. If he were, he should have a bullet instead of a whip."

"No dog shall ever — " I had begun to insist, when Felicity stood among us, a furred pelisse over her nightdress, her hair loose on her shoulders and glorious against the rich blue of the cloth.

55

"What is all this about?" she cried in wonder. "Poor De Retz? I thought Henry must be suddenly ill when I heard you all out here." Then, when my uncle had explained the situation briefly: "but you forget. De Retz is French. He's learning quickly. But all of you coming in here this way in the dead of night — " And before any of us could prevent her she was on her knees in the straw of the stall with the great brute's head in her arms, while his tail thudded his delight against the planking.

A moment before I could have knelt in adoration at her small, slippered feet. Now, at the sight of her crooning endearments over that wolfish head with its lolling mouth and eyes that rolled up at us in a look of seeming triumph, I turned away in anger.

"Give me the leash, Cousin Robert," she called. "Now, De Retz. Now, Monsieur le Cardinal, s'il vous plait. Il faut sortir pour chasser le loup avec ces deux braves gentilhommes ici. Comprenez vous mon français mauvais Americain?"

As if he did indeed understand the hound sprang to his feet, whining with eagerness.

"Be good, De Retz," said she, and put the loop of the leash into my hand. The animal strained upon it, pulling me toward the door. She stooped and printed a light kiss between his pricking ears. Squire Killian eased himself of some highflown compliment — out of the Faerie Queen, I believe — about Una and the Lion, at all events. And off we went.

"I never saw anything prettier," he said, when we had reached the street, "than the picture your young lady and this hound made together."

"Well," I growled, "there's no arguing about tastes."

"Jealous of the dog?" he gibed. "You should have seen the brute's master while you were away. I've heard the Frenchmen were marvels with the ladies but — mong Djew! — it was as good as a play to watch him trying to make up to her."

IX. — IN THE SNOWY DUSK

Up among the dead and frosty borders of old Peter's garden once more, De Retz sniffed excitedly about the steps and, nose to the ground, dragged me half the length of the path to the cold-frame. Then, lifting his head for a single deep-throated bay, he led us out by the gap in the ruined wall and through the little wood behind as fast as we could follow him. Right over Gallows Hill, with just a jog to skirt its ill-omened crown — as I remembered afterward — across Farmer Bucock's pasture and Cornelius Tourneur's eighty acres of rolling fallow we went without a check. We crossed Van Ness's Kill at the one place where a man might leap it, in the craggy depths of the Palatine Wood, and scrambled up the precipitous farther slope. The trees opened in the first clear light of dawn upon a good half-mile width of heavy plowland, over which we panted, dripping with sweat; and still the great hound strained at his leash so that my wrist ached with the pull of the loop.

The sun was over the tree-tops, and we must have been a good eight miles from home as the crow flies, when at last he stopped. A narrow border of marsh fringed the upland pond whose waters, ruffled by the breeze, spread out before us. The great beast sniffed doubtfully a few paces ahead, pulled me to the right perhaps a dozen, to the left twice as many, among the dry tussocks where the beaded cobwebs trembled in the shortening shadows and the thin ice crackled about the stalks of blighted sedge. Then he raised his head and seemed to vent his disappointment in a long-drawn howl.

We tramped round the margin and tried a cast or two upon the farther side, but quite in vain. Apparently the heat of the sun had burned up the scent. De Retz sniffed here and there perfunctorily, frankly lost interest in the whole proceeding and at last turned sullen, lay down in his tracks and refused to move until assured by the slinging of our rifles that our faces were set toward home. At that he sprang up and trotted by my side, lifting his head in a way curiously intelligent to look into our faces when either of us spoke.

This was not often. Thoroughly tired out, it was only when we had returned the hound to his loose-box and had made considerable progress with a combination of breakfast and dinner in my dining room that anything approaching a conversation was begun. And this consisted chiefly of the lawyer's elaborating what he had told me of Monsieur de Saint Loup's attentions to Felicity in the week that elapsed between my departure on my uncle's business and the Frenchman's return to New York. Monsieur de Saint Loup had been at my uncle's house on every possible occasion. He had walked with Felicity frequently. On Sunday morning he had sat in my uncle's pew and shared Felicity's prayer book. He would range the autumn woods at sunrise for the last late wildflowers and leave them with Barry to grace her plate at breakfast.

These were disturbing thoughts for me to take to bed with me that night, and the dreams which they gave rise to were so filled with dismal foreboding that I would awake in a state of depression for which I could find no remedy. My fine prospects of a fortnight ago had given place to a drab-colored vista down which I saw my uncle totter, ruined, and myself chained to some small clerk's desk here in New Dortrecht by my duty to support him through his last miserable years, while

Felicity, married to Monsieur de Saint Loup, was gone to shine in the most brilliant circles of the metropolis.

I know that I must appear sadly wanting in those qualities of courage, resource and enterprise with which a hero of romance is expected to cope with adversity. But I observe that your romantic hero is more likely to shine at rescuing the heroine from villains or shipwreck than at providing her with a suitable roof over her head and three meals a day, which was the problem for me. Daylight restored my sense of proportion, but at the same time presented me with a thought more disquieting, because more rational, than my midnight fears. And my uncle's behavior, as one day followed another, convinced me that I was not mistaken.

Each evening when we left the counting-house together the mantle of grave serenity with which he strove to hide his anxieties showed more threadbare. Each post and newsletter deepened his depression. More than once he speculated on the probable nearness of Monsieur de Saint Loup's return, adding somewhat ostentatiously that the Frenchman would bring with him the talk of the town, a thing worth more than all the news that found its way into print. Once he so far betrayed the tenor of his thoughts as to wonder aloud as to the character of the investments in which Monsieur de Saint Loup had his money, trusting it was still in the British funds, since these were most profitably convertible into cash and the present offered such lucrative opportunities for the employment of cash in this country. The notes of Barclay and Barclay at twelve months were foremost in his mind among these opportunities, I felt sure, unless a sleeping partnership were to be purchased by a prospective nephew-in-law.

For a week had not gone by before a question here, a comment there, taken together with such remarks as I have already mentioned, made the nature of his hopes quite obvious. Had I not observed that Monsieur de Saint Loup appeared to be much struck by Felicity, he asked. And at another time: Felicity seemed to find the French gentleman most agreeable. Did I not think so? They had a common interest in music, to be sure. Well, she might do worse, a portionless girl, pretty and charming though she was, he opined. And so might the Frenchman. Much worse! A noble and all that, with education and breeding, and a comfortable sum of money for a new country, doubtless; but an exile, a refugee with a price on his head, when all was said and done. Yes, Monsieur de Saint Loup might do decidedly worse than marry into one of the oldest families in America.

All this last was got off with a condescending bluster so transparent that I didn't know whether to laugh at its
58

childishness or swear at the ruin of my hopes which it presaged. It had the good effect, at least, of arousing me to a state of proper combativeness. Whatever I owed to my uncle, it was not required of me that I should sit still and let him sacrifice Felicity to this fat little Frenchman in order to save the firm of Barclay and Barclay from destruction. I knew nothing of what her opinion of the Frenchman might have become in the past two weeks. But I guessed at a capacity for self-sacrifice in her, a sense of gratitude for the home my uncle had given her, which might bring her even to make a loveless marriage, if my uncle were left free to work upon her feelings; and I determined that she should at any rate have an alternative open to her. Better poverty, with only me to wring out a scanty livelihood for us both — and for my uncle too, if it should come to that — than that she should be the plaything and convenience of this smooth foreigner.

But now I was surprised to find that my determination was more easily made than carried out. My uncle, as if he had divined my purpose, thwarted it. He would stop where our paths divided every evening and hold out his hand with a finality which precluded my keeping on with him to his own door. Busy at the counting-house the whole of every week-day, I had none of the opportunities which my rival had enjoyed, while as for the evenings, they became suddenly beset with obstacles. My uncle assigned to me tasks of night work, the compilation of figures to demonstrate the success of his business for many years past. These were for his bankers in New York, who were pressing him. And his customary reluctance to admit such a thing gave me the measure of his desire to keep me out of Felicity's company. But by the time Friday night came round, my regular night for supping with him, my blood was up, though I will not deny that I was nervous. For he was not a man to be crossed lightly.

"Why, Uncle Barclay," I exclaimed, and managed a laugh, when he would have bidden me farewell, "you have forgot. 'T is Friday."

"Friday? And what of Friday, Robert?" he asked with his exaggerated air of being willing to be set right in the unthinkable event of his being wrong.

"My night to sup with you, sir," I replied as coolly as I could. "Forgive my boldness in reminding you of it. But I would not willingly have my cousin think it strange when she heard — as she would be bound to do — that our old custom was broken the first Friday night I was in town since her arrival."

It beat him. Since he found he could not fob me off by ignoring the occasion, he yielded with a hollow graciousness:

"Why, to be sure! Your absence might seem strange to Felicity, as Barry would have laid your place at table, of course."

There would be a pleasant little surprise for me, as well, he added. Monsieur de Saint Loup had sent my cousin some new music, which undoubtedly she could be prevailed upon to perform for us.

This, in the outcome, she did, very prettily and very patiently too. For it appeared that Uncle Barclay could never hear the new airs often enough. All that mitigated my impatience was the covert glance of amused sympathy which she flashed at me when he insisted upon a third repetition of a perfectly banal piece of French Royalist sentimentality. At length, however, she rose from the harpsichord with an air of quiet decision and closed the instrument.

"Oh, but you'll never wish to hear them again if I go on singing them now," she replied to his protestations. "Besides, I've been dying for days to hear from Robert how De Retz behaved toward him on that hunt."

In exchange she told me of the progress she had made in accustoming the great hound to his environment. Every afternoon she had taken him to walk, and he had got on so rapidly that on that very day she had trusted him to go unleashed.

"You should see his lordly disregard of the yapping curs of the street," she boasted. "It is as if he were unaware of their existence. And you may be sure, though they snarl at him, they keep at a respectful distance. The children adore him, also with a proper deference to his nobility; and everybody admires him.

"So would you, Robert," she challenged the rather unsympathetic countenance with which I had listened to this panegyric, "if you had seen his behavior toward that unfortunate little Aggie Van Zile, and that savage brute of hers. The wretched child spat at him and ran away, screaming. The dog would have flown at De Retz, I believe, if old Jan hadn't reeled out of his shanty and seized him. Jan began to give me a scolding for letting a monster — so he called De Retz — run at large, but Mr. Sackville had seen the whole affair and came up just as I was beginning to grow frightened and sent him about his business."

"Curious," said I. "Aggie and her dog didn't like De Retz's master either." And I told of their encounter with Monsieur de Saint Loup on the day of his arrival.

"It is a scandal that we cannot get that child committed to an asylum," said my uncle.

Barry appeared with materials for the toddy; and when that

60

had been drunk and I rose to take my leave, my uncle was more like his usual self toward me than he had been since my return. He did indeed bid Felicity ring for Barry to show me out, but yielded at once, when she said that she would do it. In the whole world he was probably the one man least inclined by nature to be an intrigant, was our good, kind, pompous Uncle Barclay; and the warm liquor had combined with his niece's charm to conquer his resolution to keep me from speaking with her alone.

"Where and when may I talk with you privately, Robert?" she asked, when we stood at the front door. "You must think it strange that I should ask such a question, but there are certain things which I must know and which you alone can tell me. I shall be walking near Gallows Hill tomorrow about four in the afternoon. Can you join me there without our uncle's knowing of it?"

Of course I said at once that I could. She was so breathless, so changed from the gay, untroubled girl she had seemed throughout the evening; there was so much anxiety in her lovely eyes, that even had her request not fallen in exactly with my wishes, I would have complied with it.

That night the weather changed. The long succession of brisk, sparkling days and brilliant nights was broken by a wind that howled among the old brick chimneytops and set the leafless branches of the churchyard elm trees creaking and clashing over my head as I hurried home. All the next day the temperature fell steadily in one of those brief foretastes of winter which make our usual late autumn weather so doubly pleasant by contrast; low masses of gray clouds drove over us, shrouding the hilltops, turning the river leaden save when some vagrant squall lashed its waters to dull silver; the flying showers changed from rain to sleet to snow; and when I took down my hat and greatcoat at half-past three in the afternoon, preparatory to keeping my appointment with Felicity, candles were burning on all the desks in the counting-room: so dark had the day already become.

It was brighter outside, of course. Snow flew before the wind and whitened roadway and footpath, giving a false clarity to things near at hand. But dusk was deepening in the alleys. The hollows between the hills beyond the river were already lost in the gloom. In another half-hour darkness would have fallen. I hastened my steps, thankful that I would be with Felicity before it came and uneasy at the thought that even now she should be at the edge of the town, though she had the great hound to protect her. I espied the marks of her foot-steps and those of the animal as I passed old Peter's

61

house. His wall protected them from the wind just there. Farther on the drifting snow had covered them. But in the lee of Gallows Hill I found her; and the huge beast at her side bristled and growled at my approach as if he had never seen me before.

With a word and a light stroke of her hand she silenced him, I believe, but in truth I hardly know; her face flushed with walking in the wind, her eyes sparkling, so shone out at me from the little close bonnet covering her head that I was aware of nothing else. She wore the furred, blue pelisse I had first seen the night she came upon us in De Retz's stall, and out of its flaring sleeves she stretched her two gloved hands to mine in a clasp so warm that before I knew what I was doing I stooped and kissed them and kissed them again until she pulled them away.

"Felicity," I cried, hurt out of all reason, "haven't you forgiven me? Can't you trust me even yet?"

She stood silent for a moment before she answered, one hand clenched at her breast, the other in the little muff that hung by a ribbon round her neck. Then the troubled look in her eyes changed to laughter.

"Oh, Robert! As if I would have asked you to meet me here if I didn't trust you!" She drew very close to me and laid one hand on my arm. "Tell me about our uncle's affairs. Is he indeed in desperate straits? I owe him everything. I must give everything, if he is."

"Not so desperate that you must marry Monsieur de Saint Loup to extricate him," I answered. "I've no doubt he's been hinting at that. But wait until he speaks out, at least. He will not hesitate to ask you in plain language, if the time comes when the existence of the sacrosanct house of Barclay and Barclay requires that sacrifice," I added bitterly. "But, being what he is, he would like to be enabled to deceive himself into thinking that you did it of your own free will."

"But he has not had to speak out. Monsieur de Saint Loup has saved him the effort. A letter from Monsieur came by the post yesterday, making a formal proposal for my hand. Our uncle read it to me and asked me to give it my consideration. De Retz! De Retz, stop!" she broke off. "Robert, catch him!"

For the great hound, sniffing among the thickets that clothed the lower slope of the knoll, had given a short, ringing bark and dashed off, crashing through the leafless bushes, and was out of sight in an instant.

"Come quickly," she cried, pushing her way along the trail which the animal's huge leaps had left in the feathery snow. "He has never left me like this before. He might do mischief, or be accused of doing it."

Whistling and calling, we followed until, breathless, we halted in the gloom of the little wood above old Peter's house. There in the gathering darkness we had lost the trail completely. I would have been for turning back at that point in any case, for the great wolf seemed to have made that wood and the garden below it his favorite haunt. But Felicity forestalled my suggestion.

"This path will lead us to Monsieur de Saint Loup's cottage, will it not?" she asked. "Then let us return as we came. 'T is likely I shall tread that path only too often without beginning today."

"Felicity," I cried out, "you cannot mean that you will wed that fat, odious little man with his lecherous glance and growling chuckle! He would devour you, batten on your beauty. With those plump hands of his — " All my jealous imaginings were springing to my lips.

"Peace, Robert, please," she broke in upon me. "We shall not strengthen ourselves by being unfair. After all, Monsieur de Saint Loup has honored me with a proposal of marriage. This is as our uncle sees it. Not only does he waive my want of noble blood, my lack of dowry — for, save two poor servants and a few pieces of old silver and jewelry, I have nothing to bring my husband — but he offers to settle upon me the sum of twenty-five thousand dollars to be invested as our uncle shall think fit."

"And with which our good uncle will promptly purchase for you a sleeping partnership in Barclay and Barclay," I sneered; "thereby selling you exactly as if he had placed you on the auction-block at Baltimore or Charleston. But he puts an end to his business troubles."

"Oh, be fair to him," she protested. "Try to see what he sees: safety for me when all is dangerous in his affairs. If it means safety for him too, who can blame him? Not I. What must he think of me, should I refuse? How could I eat another morsel of his bread or sleep another night under his roof?"

"Felicity," I tried to interpose, but she would not hear me.

"No," she hurried on in a lower tone. "But one thing I will do, must do. When Monsieur de Saint Loup returns I will tell him that I do not love him but that, if he wishes to marry me so — as I suppose he will, from what I have heard of French marriages — "

"Felicity," I cried again, "you shall not. At least you shall wait a little. There is a chance, a good chance that I may become rich, that any day now . . . " And I poured out the whole story of old Peter's hidden money, of the lost will and the stolen coat, as Squire Killian had told it to me, and of what had happened since.

"But, Robert," she said with a sad little smile, when I paused in my pleading, "don't you see? I should have to say the same thing to you."

"That you don't love me either? I didn't dare hope you did. But you shall. And if you never should, enough of my money shall go to Uncle Barclay to save his business. I, too, owe him something. You don't suppose that I, too, wish to buy you from him?"

"Ah, Robert, I know that all your feelings are good and sweet toward me," she was beginning wistfully, her hands on my sleeve in generous understanding. Then her eyes, which had been raised to mine, shifted, widened with terror. The little wood rang with her scream:

"Look, Robert! Those eyes!"

She flung her slender body against me so that I wavered, wavered just enough. The long, snapping jaws, that would have cracked my spine just below the skull, met in my shoulder. I was hurled, face downward, in the snow. A horrid feral stench filled my nostrils; body and heavy paws pinned me down; in my ears sounded a fearful crunching, which the shocked nerves of my shoulder failed entirely to transmit to my brain.

"Run," I grunted and, as I glimpsed her feet planted firmly in the snow, "Run for help."

I twisted my left arm from under me — my right was paralyzed by the fierceness of the onslaught — I groped over the hairy, snarling face, searching for the eyes. It was the forlornest chance but, as old hunters had told me, my only one. Then something whizzed past my ear and cracked on the savage head, whizzed and cracked again. Felicity had caught up my loaded stick and was striking with all her might.

"Don't! Run!" I managed to shout. If the creature left me, crippled as I was, and turned on her, both of us were lost. I felt the jaws relax. The weight bounded from my shoulders. I leapt up, fumbling for my clasp-knife. The beast was gone.

Of what happened after that I have a cloudy recollection of the first few minutes, then none at all. I remember stumbling out of the wood with Felicity's arm about me and my sound arm round her neck, her hand clasping mine. I remember the feeling of the hot blood from my wound as it flowed over my breast and down my side. I blundered heavily and came to the ground and wished that I might never leave it and that those moments might never cease, or life cease with them. For Felicity had my head in her lap, and her kisses fell fast as her tears on my face. I remember thinking that this must be a dream. The sudden appearance of Monsieur de Saint Loup who, if he were not still in New York, could not be nearer than the packet-sloop which was due to arrive tomorrow, made me sure of it.

Carefully dressed as always, he stood looking down upon us with a smile of ironical amusement. Then he had knelt and, turning back immaculate ruffles from his soft white hands, had begun to investigate my wound. I remember the tiny popping of the severed threads as he cut away my sleeve and slashed the shoulder seam, the wintry air on my bared flesh, Felicity's gasp of horror when the full extent of the havoc was exposed. Then I must have fainted.

X. – THE SKULL OF A BLACK GOAT

I lay, delirious, for more than a week after the attack of the wolf in old Peter's wood. Afterwards I learned that Vashti shared the night watches with poor old Goody Hoskins my housekeeper, and she came often between times with soups and jellies and other delicacies from my uncle's kitchen. But in my lucid intervals I took her presence for a haunting of feverish dreams. She stood in corners, her dress and skin blending with the shadows, and the white V of her kerchief only glimmering in the feeble gleam of the night-light. Beneath the flaring points of her turban, as beneath the hieratic horns of some high-priestess' headdress, her large eyes smoldered upon me with the lights and color of the darkest carnelian.

A strange, elemental hunger consumed me, a hunger that mocked me with visions of bloody joints; and when this grew until it overcame my natural disgust for such a repast, and I was about to fling myself upon the horrid mess, Vashti's great arm would sweep it out of my sight, and she would feed me with grapes cool from my uncle's bins. But when she laid me down again, I thirsted and, to my horror, thirsted for blood. I seemed to know its taste, to remember it and long for it as I have never longed for anything in my life. I thought of animals filled with it, of people, most enticingly of all, of little children. I thought of the school in the early morning, of a lonely lane leading toward it, and a little girl with golden hair and rosy cheeks, skipping toward a thicket where I would lie hidden . . .

There was a crack of gray light between the drawn curtains. Day had begun to dawn. Stealthily I crawled from my bed, and had to be forced back into it by that great woman. She changed my bandages with such cunning that, although the wound re-opened and bled afresh, I felt no pain. Did she also strew a strange, stuffy-smelling powder over the raw flesh, and accompany the operation with droning incantations?

Ram of Abraham, our father, caught by the horns in the bushes,

As you saved little Isaac, save this child.

Black goat, Scapegoat, black Scapegoat on the mountains,
Take his curse on you, save this child.
Lord God, Lord Jesus Christ, Scapegoat of all nations,
If this arm offend thee, pluck it off,
And don't let this whole body and soul fall into your hell fire.

Was there on the folded counterpane on the foot of my bed the while a horned goat skull, so freshly stripped of its flesh that the bond showed pink along the shallow jaw, a candle flaring on either side of it, and a cross of sticks beneath?

There must have been something of all of this. For otherwise where did I get such words or such ideas — I who at that time had never heard of Voodoo worship, who had never given another thought to Felicity's telling me that Vashti was regarded as a 'conjure-woman' by those of her own race, and who had no smallest premonition of the web of dangers in which I and my dear one were already enmeshed? And there are still stronger reasons for believing in the actuality of these things, which will appear as my narrative proceeds.

Dr. Brown made a fine to-do about the changed bandages. Vashti, who had gone home to attend her mistress by the time he came, was forbidden the house. My shoulder, which had shown tardy signs of healing, was much worse. Gangrene set in; an operation became necessary; and my right arm to this day hangs limp and thin. But never again did I feel that perverted hunger, that foul thirst, which overbore even the horror it filled me with and set me planning abominations at which my soul sickened.

Other dreams took their place, from which I awoke, sweating with fright but only at wholesome, normal terrors. Or it was likely to be one dream alone, repeated four nights out of five. Felicity and I seemed to be following the tracks of De Retz through the snowy thickets round Gallows Hill again. But as we reached the skirts of the little wood the tracks changed to just such small, neat naked footprints as the one the lawyer and I had found in the ashes on old Peter's hearthstone. Again my ears rang with Felicity's warning scream. But as I whirled, bracing my frame to take the monster's onslaught, there would come only Monsieur de Saint Loup, swinging his tasselled cane, and in his eyes the same ironical amusement that had been there when last I saw him. He would be as carefully dressed as ever, save only that he minced toward us through the new-fallen snow on naked feet.

I would awake, sweating with fear, as I have said, and would lie through the long night hours, looking out into the empty street, where perhaps a watchman slouched past in his hooded greatcoat or a late reveler staggered through the strong moonlight, or towards morning the crew of some barge clumped and shouldered down to catch the dawn-wind in their great brown sails. Twice, also, I saw De Retz trot past, and each time, as if he felt my gaze upon him, the hound lifted his head and looked directly up at the dim square which the night-light must have made of my window in the blank house-front.

When, about a fortnight after my relapse, the doctor consented to my having a few visitors, Mr. Sackville was the first to call. He improvised an altar out of my washstand and gave me the Communion, smiling aside my protestations that I was in no such emergency as to justify such a thing.

"Tush, tush!" he admonished me. "I should have given it to you, had you been dying. Why not, when you are beginning to mend? Why must religion go only with the dismal things of life? It ought to be associated with the most joyful ones." And his eye rested upon me with a keen kinliness as I put the consecrated bread into my mouth, his white head nodding with such hearty approval as I was at a loss to account for till long afterwards.

Then he sat down and began to retail the gossip of the town with thoroughness and humor: how Monsieur de Saint Loup's furniture was all unpacked, and what a fine place he was making of old Peter's barren quarters; how, nevertheless, he would have no servant living under his roof, but a middle-aged widow woman who came up from the town each day to cook and clean; and how, in spite of his master's return, De Retz haunted my uncle's premises for hours each day, scorning a fine kennel at home, so as to be at hand to accompany Felicity on her walks abroad.

It was a pity the hound had not been so assiduous on the night when the wolf attacked me, I remarked rather bitterly. For my shoulder had begun to pain me, as it still did at the approach of darkness. He took me up rather quickly at that, as if he had never heard an account of the affair that fully satisfied him.

"As I understand, the hound had dashed off in pursuit of something or other, and you and Miss Paige followed, lest it should get into some mischief. It seems odd that the hound did not find the wolf before the wolf found you, does it not?"

I agreed that it did, but not so odd to me as Monsieur de Saint Loup's return the day before the packet. How had he managed that, I asked.

It appeared that a friend who was bound for Chatham by way of the Harlem valley had brought him from New York in a chaise, Mr. Sackville told me, and cutting across the hills, had set him down at his own door without entering the town at all.

To my next question the rector replied that De Retz had not reappeared until late in the evening. After I had been carried home to bed and left in the care of the doctor and Goody Hoskins, my uncle had kept the Frenchman to supper and they had sat late, talking over the news from New York which he had expected so impatiently. Monsieur had departed to his lodgings and my uncle was about to go to bed, when he heard the hound whining for admission. Since then the creature had spent some part of each day in Felicity's company and almost every night appeared at the house to guard her slumbers.

"And what says Thomas to that?" I asked.

"Oh, I understand De Retz has a shake-down in the kitchen porch now."

"And is free to run about as he likes?" I exclaimed in astonishment. "I should think his savage look would have caused effectual protests against his being at large."

On the contrary, Mr. Sackville assured me, the animal's behavior had been so circumspect that, not only was he tolerated, but people felt that the streets were safer at night for his presence. Monsieur de Saint Loup was confident of the hound as a protector against any more forays by the wolf and considered him a far more effectual remedy than the reward offered by the town council.

"I cannot see that his master gets much good of him."

"Now that comment brings us to a curious thing," Mr. Sackville replied. "When Monsieur de Saint Loup goes abroad the hound is always at home. When he sups at your uncle's or walks with Miss Felicity, for instance, De Retz is absent, on guard evidently at old Armitage's against anybody who might be tempted to investigate either the old tales of buried wealth or the Frenchman's new luxuries. 'T is quite amazing how they seem to share and divide that duty."

Of other news which I cared about the clergyman had little — or little that he chose to tell, I suspected.

"Business?" he parried. "Bad enough, I hear, but not so bad that Barclay and Barclay will not weather the storm." Then, thinking doubtless that he might safely set my anxieties at rest by doing so, he added, "Your uncle tells me that he has been able to make certain private arrangements as to credit that will tide him over nicely."

"What!" I exclaimed. "Already?"

The look on his brave old face told me that he caught all the implications of my bitter cry. He paused for several moments before replying.

"Monsieur de Saint Loup seems an excellent gentleman," he said at last. "After all, simply because you and I don't happen to take to him — "

"Surely my uncle might have waited to make inquiries. A letter to our minister at Paris — Or did he write to the French consul in New York?"

"I gathered that your uncle dared not wait," Mr. Sackville answered soberly. He rose at that and took an almost hurried departure. From my bed I watched him down the bare, gray street. His head was bent, his hands clasped behind him, a very different figure from the erect, striding man that usually paid his parochial calls.

Meanwhile I had seen nothing of those nearest to me, and dearest. My uncle had looked in on me each of the two Sunday afternoons when I lay comatose or delirious, and had sent Barry to inquire every morning and every night. That he should not have come since I began to mend did not surprise me. I knew that he was as fond of me as ever, and really fond: only to break the ordered regularity of every day and evening for a sick nephew was unthinkable; and on the first Sunday when I was lucid he had dined with Monsieur de Saint Loup. But it hurt and alarmed me to have the days go by and bring no visit from Felicity. Surely our relationship, even had she lacked the substantial Vashti for duenna, even had I been but half so sick and helpless as I was, might have quieted any fear of scandal, I thought. And remembering the bitter sweetness of those tears and kisses she had rained upon my face up there in old Peter's wood, I knew that it must have taken more than the fear of that to keep her from me. Was it that she had something to tell me that I was not yet strong enough to bear?

She came the next Sunday with my uncle. The snow of that early storm had all vanished since in a few hot suns, and it was one of those bright, dry, blustering November days that made even my sluggish blood quicken as I lay in bed, and set my thoughts running on what it would be like to have a good horse under me or to be tramping the hills. Through the small square panes of my window I could see masses of white cloud scudding across a sky of intense blue, each chimney with its whisk of smoke, and the bare tree-tops swaying. The rays of the declining sun turned my dull room bright. The faded chintzes of my bed curtains, at my windows and on the chairs, were gay with it. My heart beat fast to hear old Goody panting up the stairs ahead of my callers to tell me who they were and put me a little to rights in order to receive them. Behind her came the thud of heavy pads and the click of claws, and De Retz, head erect and great tail swaying, followed her into the room.

My uncle, calling heartily from the door, stepped aside for Felicity to enter — and all went suddenly dull in the hard brilliance of this girl who, always before this, had seemed to shed a generous radiance on everything about her. Now she was like the diamond, that draws all light to itself. You will have seen the same thing in any young girl who has engaged herself to marry brilliantly without love. Her eyes were bright, her cheeks vivid; her smile flashed: but it was with the chill splendor of a sunlit day in winter.

"Why, Cousin, how well you look!" she cried and, crossing swiftly to my bed, she dropped upon my forehead a kiss as light and cold as a snowflake. "I had no hope of finding you so far recovered. Had we but known, Uncle Barclay, we might have brought Monsieur de Saint Loup with us as he desired."

"True," my uncle agreed, sinking into the chair Goody Hoskins placed for him, "Monsieur desired me to give you his compliments, Robert."

There followed a little pause after that, awkward for my uncle doubtless but nothing to me who seemed to hear my heart breaking in my breast: Felicity sat so still and beautiful, and to all appearance so serene. To keep from looking at her I watched De Retz. He had seated himself in the corner nearest her and, with forelegs lifted from the floor, held his great body nearly upright, as if to show how far his intelligence raised him above his animal state. His tongue lolled between the rows of his white teeth, and his eyes shifted from her to me with a burning intensity.

"You will be glad to know that my business difficulties are less acute, Robert," my uncle said at length.

"The rector told me you had discovered a private source of credit, sir," I replied.

My uncle had the grace to be flustered.

"Yes, yes, a private source," he stammered. "And I am glad of this early opportunity to tell you of it, since at my death — and at my age death draws near, my boy — the house of Barclay and Barclay will be yours and your cousin's here."

"And Monsieur de Saint Loup's, I suppose," I burst out, too indignant to simulate any respect for the tawdry display of emotion for which he had paused.

"Ah!" he ejaculated, becoming ponderously arch, with a glance at Felicity. "As to that you must still seek information other than mine. But Monsieur de Saint Loup volunteered last week to honor my demand notes up to thirty thousand dollars and at my request did so immediately for ten thousand."

"And you cannot well continue to remain obdurate after that, can you, Cousin?" I asked, turning upon Felicity — God forgive me — with a sneer I was at little pains to hide.

"Could any girl resist such evidence of wealth and generosity in a suitor, Cousin?" she returned, her delicate chin lifted. "I only heard of it on Wednesday, but I could not do less than promise Monsieur de Saint Loup his answer tonight."

"I wish you all such happiness as will certainly be yours," said I.

"Why, come now. That's splendid," cried my uncle in high good humor. "I may say, that's gallant of you, Robert. Spoken like a gentleman! How you would take this news was, I confess, the cause of some uneasiness to me. Ignorant of the exact state of your feelings, I feared, however . . . "

He had more to say in the same strain, but if I heard it, I have forgotten it now. At the strength of his wilful dullness Felicity's glance and mine had met in a look of astonishment, and instantly my whole body glowed with joy. For her eyes, which had been lowered since her proud rejoinder to my gibe, were brimming with tears, and I understood how her gay manner and brilliant look had been assumed for my uncle's reassurance — a thing which only so great a fool as I would have missed from the first.

"You forget our other news, I think, dear uncle," said she, when finally he had ceased to embroider his satisfaction at my behavior.

"Ah, to be sure," he exclaimed. "All our troubles draw to an end together. The wolf, Robert — your old enemy — traced to its lair — dead, my boy — shot by a farmer some fifteen miles from here."

"But not without a final touch of the grotesque which was characteristic of the creature. Don't forget that, Uncle Barclay."

"A touch of the grotesque — characteristic? I had not been aware, my dear — "

"I mean the black goat," she interrupted. "About two or three weeks ago, Cousin Robert, the dead body of a black goat was discovered near the river bank. It had been decapitated and the head could not be found. Now I call that grotesque, don't you? The body had not been touched — not any part of it devoured, I mean."

"The wolf," said my uncle, "was evidently not in search of food on any of his forays hereabouts. He was a killer, killing for the mere lust for slaughter. Old frontiersmen are acquainted with that type."

"But has it not been strange, sir," Felicity asked, "that there have been no reports of depredations among the sheepfolds and cattle pens of the neighborhood? Apparently the beast came and went fasting."

"It broke its fast very effectually on the live stock of the farmer who shot it, at all events," my uncle replied. But I confess that I did not pay the best attention to this

71

interchange. My mind ran back to that night in my delirium.

"Black goat, Scapegoat, black Scapegoat on the mountains, Save this child . . . "

And the senile grin of that shallow-jawed skull.

It had not been a dream then. Vashti, in her own poor ignorant estimation, had indeed wrought a spell on me. But why had I seemed to her to lie in need of spells?

"You are satisfied that the creature shot is in fact the marauder?" I asked, discovering that a silence had fallen and both of them were looking at me.

"Monsieur de Saint Loup isn't," Felicity replied.

"But he is used to France and the protected game of all kinds in the royal forests and the like," said my uncle. "He does not realize how unlikely it is that there should be two such creatures at large."

But after my visitors were gone, after I had finished my supper and Goody had left me with trimmed candles to my book, it was the goat's head and Vashti's motive for using it that engaged my thoughts. Not that the speculation did not seem an idle one; but if I kept my mind firmly fixed upon it, at least I was safe from visions of the hard brilliance of Felicity's beauty or — worse still — of her brimming eyes. And suddenly, as with the eye of memory I scanned that queer assortment of objects which had lain on my counterpane, the slender skull, the cross of sticks, the flaring candles, I saw another collection of grotesque oddments: the little heap on the floor of my uncle's stable outside De Retz's stall, bones, bits of steel and colored glass and that wad of hair, crowned by the still bloody cock's head. I remembered Thomas's feeble excuse for its presence there. I recalled what Felicity had told me of Vashti's reputation of 'conjure-woman' among her own people: and my mind made between the two the connection which in a mood less idle it would have ignored as too fantastic for even a passing thought.

Had the great hound been the object of both incantations then? In the dark mind of this poor negress was I the victim of its diabolical powers? Was it De Retz, and no marauding wolf, that had held the town in terror, felled me in old Peter's wood, just missed me that midnight with Squire Killian in the miser's garden, and slain the little, drab lawyer's clerk on the very steps which it had stained with the blood of old Peter himself? Was that Vashti's belief?

But, if so, how did she get round the fact that De Retz did not arrive in town until many days after old Peter's bloody taking-off? Mildly entertained by this extravagant idea, I let my thoughts play. Granted that the great hound could have had nothing to do with old Peter's death, the killing of Nero, the chase after the rector and the weird appearance of the wolf outside my uncle's drawing-room window, it might be guilty of all the rest — if it could be true, as old Thomas believed, that it came and went at will through the latched gate and bolted doors of my uncle's stable.

Suddenly, illogically, I burned with regret that I could not have searched the tracks in the falling snow that night when I was struck down. Would they have showed that De Retz had doubled, crept back upon us as we stood in our passionate talk . . . ? Where, as a matter of fact, had the great hound gone that night so as to miss the wolf and neither scent nor be scented by it? Vashti, I could guess, had asked herself that question and, untroubled by the restrictions of rational thought, had answered it easily. De Retz's having led the lawyer and me for miles on the track of the wolf would be no more to her than another instance of his cunning. And as if my effort to enter her mind and think her thoughts had caused her to materialize out of the quiet air of my room, all at once she stood before me.

I cannot say that I raised my eyes and found her there. I believe that I had been staring straight in front of me, lost in my fancies. I heard no sound, was conscious of no movement. Simply, where there had been only a shadowy space framed between the valance of the canopy, the carved posts of my bed and the folded counterpane at my feet, she stood now in her bright turban and crossed kerchief, her strong hands folded before her, her luminous eyes brooding upon my face.

XI. — VASHTI'S COUNSEL

I had not ceased to stare at her before she spoke.

"Henry and I are going to be sent away from here, Mr. Farrier, sir; and I make bold to come to tell you good-bye," she said in her deep tones. And at sound of her voice all the fantastic ideas which I had been attributing to her seemed doubly absurd: her bearing was so full of quiet dignity.

"Yes, sir," she replied to my expression of astonishment, "Monsieur de Saint Loup insist we must go — must be sold South, he says. But Miss F'lic'ty don't allow that, anyhow. She send us to her cousins in Virginia as a gift. And I make bold to ask you that you always be a good friend to her, Mr. Farrier, sir, whatever happen. Whatever happen," she repeated solemnly, as I would have begun to reassure her. "Don't ever do anything to put it out of your power to be close at hand to help her in her need."

"But, Vashti, what could ever happen to cause me to do such a thing?" I asked, bewildered.

73

"Your anger, sir, and the young, strong pride of you and her, and your broken heart."

"Over her marriage to Monsieur de Saint Loup, you mean?" I asked with a sort of fierce joy at the pain it cost me to put the abomination into words.

"Yes, sir. That is what I mean. But you just always remember she don't do what she want to do, only what she must do for her uncle, like she send Henry and me away."

"Then," said I, "I shall have to be friendly with Monsieur de Saint Loup, if I am to be near enough to her to help her. Is that what you mean?"

"Yes, sir, friendly with him. That is it. At least act so friendly with him as you can."

"I doubt if he will let me, Vashti."

"Yes, he will surely let you, Mr. Farrier, sir," she replied with eager confidence. "He will like you to be friendly, so you will see him often with Miss F'lic'ty engaged to him and after she is married to him. He know you love Miss F'lic'ty, he guess she love you; and it give pleasure to a man like he is to see you miserable together while he look on and know he has her to do with what he like."

"But he must know you would be miserable, too, if she were unhappy," I objected. "Yet he is sending you away."

At that her expression changed. The look of almost childlike wistfulness vanished. Her mouth opened in a grim, noiseless laugh, while her eyes frowned.

"He is scared of me. Monsieur de Saint Loup fears me. I put a spell on him, Mr. Farrier, sir — a spell that couldn't hurt a good man but can fill the heart of a bad man with fear. And he felt that fear. He has lived in Hayti when he is young. So when he feel the fear he know there is a spell on him and he search and find what I put under his doorstep and come to Mr. Barclay and Miss F'lic'ty about it, very angry — and very afraid, too, underneath — and say we must go because we have insulted him with that spell. And if Mr. Barclay don't sell us South, he must pay back the money Monsieur de Saint Loup let him have for his business."

"And you really did put a spell on him, Vashti? Why?"

"To drive him off, Mr. Farrier, sir, so he couldn't come near Miss F'lic'ty."

"You put one on his hound, too, didn't you?" I asked, and wondered what significance that simple question could have for her. For she visibly started, her hands moved with an impulsive gesture, her eyes kindled and her lips opened — but only to close more firmly. So long was she silent that I repeated my question.

"That hound is wicked like his master," she said at length,

74

adding with sudden passion, "Ain't any use to tell you the wickedness of them, Mr. Farrier. Ain't any use to tell some people some things. When they see them they won't believe them. How can they believe them when you only tell them?"

"I could believe a great deal against Monsieur de Saint Loup, Vashti," I said with a bitter smile.

"Yes, sir. Yes, sir. But not like this, not like what I know about him. You just do like I say, Mr. Farrier, sir. Be friendly with him and watchful and always round so Miss F'lic'ty can reach you. This is the best you can do. That is all you can do. Wish you good-bye, Mr. Farrier, sir."

"Tell me somethng, Vashti," I said, as she turned to go. "You put a spell on me, didn't you, when I lay here very sick? Why did you do that?"

She did not come back to the foot of my bed to answer me, only turned her head so that her chin almost touched the splendid curve of her shoulder, and fixed me with inscrutable eyes.

"To stop your bad dreams, Mr. Farrier, sir," she said in a tone so low it barely reached me. "That kind of hound bite like you got give people terrible dreams. You have not had them any more, have you? No. That is the reason for that spell I put on you. Dreams!"

The door closed noiselessly behind her, and I heard neither her feet on the stairs nor any sound of her leaving the house.

From the rector I had the whole squalid story of their dismissal before half the week was out. Because I was now improving rapidly — save that no strength came back into my arm — Mr. Sackville did not attempt to hide the troubled state of mind into which these events had thrown him. He had been bidden to supper that Sunday evening and had awaited with my uncle and Felicity the tardy arrival of Monsieur de Saint Loup. The Frenchman burst in upon them at last in the greatest disorder. He had brought with him various articles to support his charge, tore open a loosely wrapped paper parcel and displayed a goat's skull, a cross of twigs, a broken knife-blade, nails, bits of glass and a wad of hair which, he insisted, was combings from his own head.

He arranged these oddments as he said he had found them beneath his doorstep, speaking the while with a passion which would have been laughable but for the terror it failed utterly to mask. He had been in Hayti, he cried; he had seen the necromancy practiced by the blacks of that island; the intent of these things was murder. Placed in such combination they were used only against a sorcerer; and Mademoiselle Felicity's femme-de-chambre was the only person hereabouts who could be possessed of the knowledge so to use them. She must go, must go to hard labor in the South, and with her the coachman, who was doubtless her confederate.

"Not a pretty scene, I assure you," the rector went on with a sigh and a shake of his long white hair. "But there was worse to come. I mean the sight of your uncle's truckling to the fat little bully. When Mr. Barclay said that he would investigate, he was told that the investigation was over, that unless the wretched negroes left on Tuesday's packet his notes would be presented for immediate payment. He then sought refuge in saying that the negroes were not his but Miss Paige's — God help him, poor man! She — brave girl that she is — brought in what dignity and decency could be injected into so sordid a business. Her servants should be sent away, certainly, she said; but they were not to be sold to hard labor. Her cousins in Virginia would give them a comfortable home, though they could not afford to pay her for them.

"Our French friend would have liked to make an issue of that, I feel sure. His mouth opened for another tirade, but she met his glance with such a look of quiet determination that he closed it again and merely shrugged. Meanwhile your unhappy uncle had begun to save his face in that way of his which we know so well. 'I trust, Monsieur de Saint Loup,' says he severely, now that nothing could be accomplished by severity, 'I trust you understand the financial sacrifice your demand entails upon my niece.'

"And what do you suppose Monsieur has to say to that?" Mr. Sackville continued, his voice a little shrill with his indignation. "Says he, 'Mistaire Barclay, I have nevaire been interested in the subject of your niece's dowry.' "

"And she could accept him after that, on that very evening!" I burst out. "Oh, I know what she tells herself: that she does it to save her uncle from ruin; that he gave her a home, and so on. But if Saint Loup hadn't money, if she might not some day be called countess, I wonder — "

"But if he hadn't money, my boy, he couldn't save your uncle's business. Nay. You must credit her with the purest motives." The rector was warm in his championship. "But I sometimes wonder whether a young life ought ever to be sacrificed for an old one. I wonder so much that, if these were the times of two hundred years ago, I should be tempted not to permit it. I could use the degraded superstitions of the flock I should then have under me to drive Monsieur de Saint Loup out of the country, a penniless fugitive from justice.

"Only consider," he went on; and as I noted how the indignation had died out of his voice and a whimsical note sounded in it, I guessed that he was bent on distracting the thoughts of both of us from the painful subject which had
76

engaged them. "There are certain coincidences between Monsieur de Saint Loup's actions and movement and the depredations of that great wolf. Its first outrage occurs on the first night after his arrival in town. Old Peter's corpse bleeds at his approach. He takes old Peter's house, which is so conveniently made vacant for him."

"And he expressed the certainty he would have it the day he came," I chimed in, amused.

"Better and better! I hadn't known of that. But to resume. I entertain Miss Felicity at your uncle's two nights later with an account of werewolves in Monsieur's presence, thus showing him that one member of this community – and probably only one – knows about such creatures. Meanwhile I have twitted him about the bleeding of the corpse. Also the wolf has killed my big Nero. That night the wolf ambushes me, pursues, and all but succeeds in slaying me. You will recall that we met Monsieur later that night when we were prowling about with the watch. He had been up to look at his new property, he told us. Well, he leaves town, and there are no more outrages until his hound arrives. You will remember how explicit Monsieur was that night about the creature's being named after the Cardinal de Retz and not after the unfortunate lycanthropist as I assumed. One might have thought him sensitive on that point.

"The hound arrives, I say – a beast of strength equal to any atrocity; and the outrages begin again. De Retz adores Miss Felicity, dislikes me, hates you. The horses fear him. The servants are in terror of him. Bolts and bars will not keep him in at night, they say. Other dogs loathe, but dare not attack him. Meanwhile old Peter's house is haunted but – by another coincidence – not until after De Retz's arrival. See how easily I could have set my sixteenth century congregation ravening at his heels!"

"How are you so sure of your dates?" I asked curiously.

"I keep a diary – one of my defences against the sin of idleness. I didn't like this fellow from the moment I set eyes on him. I distrusted him. God forgive me, but in the words of the Psalmist I fear I sought occasion against him. I noted down such of his movements as I heard of. De Retz was interesting in himself."

"There is an actual possibility which your data do bring out," said I; and I told him what had occurred to me: that although old Peter's death, the slaughter of Nero and so forth, must have been the work of the wolf, the killing of Squire Killian's clerk and the two attacks upon me could have been made by the hound.

"Not unless you believe that De Retz can unbar doors," he

77

objected, "that you and Miss Felicity could mistake for a wolf the dog that had been in your company only a half hour before; to say nothing of the fact that a huge timber wolf has actually been shot within striking distance of the town."

"You're right," I admitted. "Vashti's talk of spells has blunted my sense of the rational."

"That is where she had the advantage of us," he said, smiling. "She ignores the rational, crosses the borders of possibility at will. Well, it has made an amusing diversion and a harmless one, so long as we keep it to ourselves — although I feel like a dog for indulging in it. I'm ashamed to tell you the sum he gave me, as he put it, for my poor."

He rose and began to put on his cloak, still talking:

"But, oh, what a case I should make against him if we were back in the days of old King Jamie the Witch-catcher! I have never seen hound and master together, for instance, nor do I hear that anybody else ever has. Of course, one never could, if the two were merely different appearances of the same person."

I did not reply at once. Unknown to me while we talked my mind had been running on the facts which he had set in their proper order, and at that moment it presented me with an idea so startling that I very nearly burst out with it. But it was an idea for Killian's consideration, not the rector's, for it involved the story of my inheritance, which had begun by this time to seem so unlikely to come to any issue that shame kept me silent about it. So, when he paused, I suggested humorously:

"Why don't you comment to Monsieur himself on the fact that he and his dog are never seen together?"

"Because I mean to keep friends with him by every means possible, since he is to marry your cousin," he answered gravely. "And I implore you to do likewise. I have a feeling, Robert, that it may be well for her if good friends like us are in a position to keep near her."

With which ominous echo of Vashti's counsel he left me.

Squire Killian came in to see me the next morning. By this careful avoidance of the topic I guessed that he had heard the news of Felicity's engagement and understood all that it meant to me, and that his call was really a visit of condolence. His only allusion to it could hardly have been more vague, however.

"Now about that inheritance of yours," he began, his face losing something of its look of a withered pickle as the smile of greeting faded from it. "Something has got to be done about it, or you'll miss what would make it most worth

78

having. Also the court is after me. They think I have had time enough to produce a will, if there is one. They want to know why they shouldn't proceed to settle the business on the theory that the old man died intestate."

"Listen," said I, "I had an idea. It may not amount to much. It may strike you as perfectly crazy. But I think it is worth something as an hypothesis, at least. Who could have found out where that money is?"

"Nobody."

"What about the haunter?"

"He'd have begun to make off with it by now and left some trace. But I've kept my eye on things up there, and there isn't a sign."

"But suppose he didn't need to make off with it, that it was most convenient for him to leave it where he found it. Who could that be?"

"Anybody with a foot as slim and delicate as a girl's, who chooses to go barefoot on cold, bare boards, I suppose."

That graveled me for the moment, I admit. In building up my theory I had forgotten that foot track, our only first-hand evidence that the prowler in the green coat actually existed. I said stubbornly, however:

"Leaving that aside, who would be most content, supposing he were dishonest, to let the money lie where old Peter left it? Who would be in a position to play ghost most easily and with the least fear of detection?"

"Do you mean Monsieur de Saint Loup?"

"Why not?"

"Well, first because the ghost appeared while Saint Loup was in New York."

"Suppose that there was no foundation for the story to begin with, that it was merely the sort of yarn that gets started in such circumstances, and that Saint Loup, on hearing of it, saw how he could use it to keep off intruders."

"You will also have to assume that Saint Loup got into the house and obtained possession of the coat while the laborer was gone to fetch the coroner. What would the Frenchman be doing, prowling about up there at dawn after his very first night in town? Moreover, my boy, you may as well assume that, if you are right, old Peter's will is nothing but ashes long before this time."

"I don't think so," I replied. If Vashti were right, if Saint Loup's enjoyment of his young betrothed was to be heightened for him by watching the torments of a disappointed suitor, he was not the man to resist the pleasure of keeping by him an instrument which would make that suitor rich and a powerful rival, should it come into the proper

79

hands. But I had no wish to explain all that to the lawyer, naturally, and was relieved when he paid no attention to my dissent.

"No," he said. "That leads us to nothing. But late last night I thought of one place where I haven't looked — dolt that I am!"

"At least," I interrupted to my future sorrow, "look there secretly, if possible. Pay so much attention to my suspicion. Don't go up there and ask Saint Loup if you may search. You'll find nothing if you do; that I'll warrant."

"He shall know nothing of it," he promised. "And if I find the money, I expect to find the green coat with it."

"And where will you look?" I asked eagerly.

But my question was destined never to be answered by good, queer Squire Killian.

"When I tell you, you will wonder, as I have done, that we never thought of it, and you will be as sure as I am that we are right," he was beginning, when Goody Hoskin's heavy breathing sounded outside my door.

"It's Monseer — the French gentleman," she wheezed in accompaniment to her knock.

"I'll give you news of it in a day or two," said the lawyer quickly. But even that might have been heard by Monsieur de Saint Loup: so immediately did his entrance follow the announcement of his name.

I braced myself for what instinctively I felt would be an ordeal — though how hard a one I did not suspect — and found a new Monsieur de Saint Loup before me. He had been democratic, loquacious, hail-fellow-well-met on the day of his arrival. I had seen him stately, subtle, and touched with melancholy pride in my uncle's drawing-room. Now, crowned with success, his position in the community established, he was the man of the world, the urbane aristocrat, and breezy with the condescension that springs from high good humor. I was "his kind young friend," intelligence of whose steady recovery rejoiced him. He greeted Killian and paid his compliments to the skill of "the clever Doctor Brown," as if the one were the country notary, the other the village apothecary, on his estates.

"I beg you will not go until I can go with you," he said when the lawyer would have taken his departure; but there was more of command than request behind the smooth tones. "My marriage contract is to be drawn this morning, and Mr. Barclay and I are agreed that none but you shall draw it for us. Meanwhile I linger only to receive the promise of my good friend Robert here that he will — how is it you say? — stand up with me before the altar? And that, I think you will not
80

refuse? No. I thought not. Nevertheless I thank you.

"And to think, my good Killian," he ran on when I had accepted his invitation with as much grace as between bitterness and astonishment I could manage, "to think that at first I looked upon this young man as a rival! Where, think you, were his sensibilities, that he let an old rake like me carry this young beauty off from beneath his nose?" And he ended with his low growl of a chuckle.

A rake he looked, but by no means an old one, with his cheeks darkly flushed, his eyes sparkling, and the tiny beads of sweat along his upper lip. If Killian had not filled the pause with the conventional congratulations, I doubt if I could have carried off my part in the scene just then. This was having the knife twisted in the wound with a vengeance, and there was an ironical undertone in his voice which made me well aware that he enjoyed to the full the pain of each stab that he inflicted.

"Your lovely cousin will be delighted that you are to have so intimate a part in our nuptials," he told me as he wrung my hand at parting.

Squire Killian followed him out, but turned to fling a final word over his shoulder:

"I'll report on your affair in a day or two, Mr. Farrier."

Was it Monsieur de Saint Loup's manner of perfect indifference to these words that me feel sure he had heard and noted them?

XII. – THE NADIR

My tide of fortune was to sink far lower, but never were my hopes, my courage, my mere common manliness to be so completely at the ebb as in the next few days. I was still pitiably weak in body, and the contemplation of my useless right arm threw me into fits of depression from which even my constant speculations as to the hiding place of old Peter's money failed to rouse me.

"I'll report on your affair in a day or two," Squire Killian had promised at parting. And so confident had been his tone that for a while my spirits were high. Let him find the will and the miser's hoard and our troubles would be over, my uncle's business entrenched behind a hundred thousand dollars of hard money, Felicity free to bestow her beauty as her heart should dictate. But when the third day had passed and I learned in response to a note, with which I sent Goody Hoskins to the lawyer's office, that he had been called to Albany on business that might keep him away for a fortnight, I sank into despair.

That was the day, moreover, on which Barry brought me my invitation for the supper at which my uncle would formally announce the engagement of his niece to Monsieur de Saint Loup. With the gusto of the old servant who rejoices in everything that reflects splendor on his master's house, good, stupid Barry spared me no detail of the fine preparations which the prospective bridegroom was making for the reception of his bride, the silk hangings for the bedchamber, the painted bed, the elegant posting-chaise and black horses which were to carry the couple on a wedding journey to New York. This vehicle had even a set of runners to replace the wheels, in case heavy snows should have fallen before their return, and the carriage and horses were already at the tavern stable, since there was no proper stabling at old Peter's place.

"Heavy snows before their return?" I asked. "Before their departure, you mean, don't you?"

"Not likely, Mr. Robert; middle of December, you know," he replied; and in response to my explanation of astonishment he told me that, while the wedding day had not been definitely set, he had gathered it was to be well before Christmas. "Mounseer" seemed very keen to push it forward.

It was owing to the effect of this news upon me, I imagine, that Doctor Brown not only permitted but advised me to begin going out of doors, so long as I was careful not to overfatigue myself and to confine my walks to the sunny hours. So the next afternoon, muffled in my greatcoat and leaning more heavily than I liked upon my walking stick, I went creeping about wherever I saw the greatest prospect of sunshine and the least of exposing my crippled arm in its sling to the stares of passersby and the commiseration of acquaintances. But I had not gone far when there came a clatter of hoofs behind me, the roll of wheels and, hailing me jovially, the voice I cared least to hear in all the world. Next moment the handsome new posting-chaise was drawn up at the curb beside me and Monsieur de Saint Loup had sprung out of it and stood, holding the door for me to enter.

He had just called for me at my house, he explained; he was engaged in trying out a candidate for postboy. Would I join him? We would see how the fellow managed the stiff hill up to his "cottage," and there, before we tried him on the descent, would fortify our courage with a glass of Madeira and a biscuit. Besides, he wishes to show me the house. I had not seen it since old Peter's day, had I? There were certain embellishments in anticipation of a celestial event.

Never has my temper endured a greater strain than in the hour that followed. I was subjected to the subtlest torment. Yet not only must I bear it, but bear it so perfectly as to appear to be unconscious of it. With a hypocritical assumption that cousinly affection was the strongest feeling that could exist between Felicity and me, I was called upon, as one man of the world might call upon another, to consider her taste, examine her disposition, and listen to rhapsodical exclamations upon her beauty, which, though never transgressing the canons of good taste, were delivered with an anticipatory relish that made the blood sting in my cheeks. And while all this was gotten off with an air of total innocence of its stirring in me any emotion stronger than those natural to a relative in the circumstances, there lurked behind the gay glance of those dark eyes a deadly mockery, there rang beneath the light tones of his voice a note of cruel raillery that made me well aware of his knowledge of my impotence and of his delights in the torture he was inflicting on me. Nay, more! For I felt that he understood my purpose in enduring it and my reasons for doing so. When, for instance, he was emphatic in his regrets that Doctor Brown would not allow me to expose myself to the night air by coming to the announcement supper that evening, he made me feel that what he chiefly regretted was that he should miss the sight of my face at the moment which would mark the frustration of all my hopes.

When at last we alighted before his house I was like a man fainting upon the rack: all my thought, all my being, were so absorbed in the single task of keeping my lips sealed. And as such a one might fix his mind upon some oath of conspirators whom he was being tortured to betray, I fixed mine on Vashti's admonition and Mr. Sackville's unconscious echo of it. The release from the secluded intimacy of the carriage, however, was as if the wheels and ropes of some dreadful engine had been relaxed. My mind expanded to take in the smartly painted gate and the repairs upon the wall, the freshly graveled paths and cleaned flowerbeds. And although there was no actual mitigation of his cruelty, though he spared me, at least by implication, no detail of his future bliss as he foresaw it, I was free to move about, to place the length of the newly polished floor between us in examining a picture or the pattern of the hangings, to look out and comment on the view.

The principal room, which I had last seen cluttered with bales and packing cases, was now, as nearly as it could be made, a drawing-room in the French manner, consoles and pier glasses between the richly curtained windows, delicate sofas and armchairs in silk; only at the farther end a small dining table and a dresser glimmered with old silver and was bright with the ware of Sevres. The hearth in whose ashes Killian and I had found that inexplicable naked footprint was guarded by a brazen fender of exquisite cutting. Brass and-irons matched this, and on the shelf above, a clock like a little temple of the hours ticked with soft swiftness.

83

Of the three smaller rooms which the house contained, beside the kitchen, one had the simple comforts suitable for madame's femme-de-chambre. He paused to ask my opinion of the maid whom he had purchased in New York to take the place of Vashti; and when I told him that I hadn't seen her, he dropped a word or two about her grace and beauty.

"The woman from the town will continue to come to cook and clean," he went on. "But a lady's maid should be able to manage the morning chocolate, which I always enjoy most in bed, especially when I have a beautiful companion to share it with me. Here," he added, opening the next door, "is the place I have dedicated to myself."

My first thought was that the room had not been finished: it looked, so nearly as bare as when the lawyer and I had shed the fluctuating light of our candle upon it in search of the mysterious maker of the footprint. It contained, in fact, the merest necessaries of living, and beyond them little more: a well-worn saddle on a rough frame, a great armoire for clothes, a small desk with a case of dueling pistols on it, and over the fireplace a rude rack which held a fowling piece, a pair of horse pistols in their holsters and various whips and straps.

"You wonder at its simplicity, I see," he went on. "You think it temporary, perhaps? I assure you, it is not. I mean to keep it so in order to remind me even in my bliss that I am an exile. I shall use it as my dressing room; and to come out of those warm young arms into this will do so, will it not? Also it serves as a convenient storage place for certain things hardly pleasing to a young bride yet precious to me for their associations. This for instance."

Advancing to the fireplace, he took down from above it one of the straps that hung there, and placed it in my hand. Of a singular softness and pliancy, a delicate whitish-gray in color, it was about three feet long and an inch in width. Its texture in my fingers was like no other leather I had ever touched.

"That," he explained, smiling at my puzzled examination of it, "is a strip of human skin taken from the living body of a beautiful Circassian female slave. The property of a certain pasha in Senegal who once honored me with his friendship, she had been detected in an infidelity with one of his guards. The man he fed, living, to his lions. The girl, as an example to the rest of his harem, he punished by causing her skin to be removed from her living body in a single strip as one peels an apple — a most delicate and curious operation."

"You mean you saw it?" I cried, aghast.

"But yes," he stooped to pick up the horrid relic, which had slipped through my fingers to the floor, and lifted his face to mine with a smile. "It was a singular token of his confidence in me to include me in what was so entirely a family affair."

"And you sat and actually watched it?"

"But, mon gars, my refusal to do so wouldn't have helped the miserable girl and would have imperiled what was for me a valuable friendship. It has a charming texture even now, has it not? But think of its rosy warmth beneath the lover's caress."

He kept drawing the strip through his fingers as he spoke, as if the feeling of it stirred some voluptuous memory, and hung it carefully back in its place before closing and locking the door behind him.

"De Retz shall sleep in there, with the door open, on any night when I must be abroad. It does no harm for a young wife to have a guardian that is known to be not altogether amenable to reason." Again he smiled at me.

"Shall we now visit the room which I have kept for the last, since it is the raison d'etre of the whole, the bride's apartment?" he asked, throwing open the door and standing aside for me to enter.

The way he had held it back had warned me that he meant this for the ultimate torture. But, while the suspense resulting from this delay heightened the effect he wished to make, I had been given an opportunity to steel myself against it. Barry's clumsy stories, and the rest of the house itself, moreover, had prepared me for what I should see. So I could let my eyes travel from the low, French bed with its carved cupids and garlanded headboard, across the rose-hued carpet into which the feet sank noiselessly as into moss, to the gold-and-ivory intimacies of the toilet table and the cloudy beauties of a lace robe de chambre that lay ready on the silk cushions of a chaise longue, as coolly as if the whole had been no more than the display of a fashionable upholsterer.

His eyes never left my face, missed no movement of my glance.

"She will be pleased by this, you think?" And lifting the robe de chambre from where it lay, he pressed it to his lips quickly twice and remained smiling at me above the lacy billows with a mockery which, perhaps, would have tantalized beyond endurance a Frenchman in my place. But the action struck me as grotesque to the point of absurdity. I believe I

"Well," I drawled, "you must not forget that American ladies, especially those who have lived chiefly in the country, as my cousin has done, are likely to be wearied by luxuries so elaborate as to be troublesome. That is my only criticism of the whole room, since you ask it. In itself, it is, of course, perfect."

It was joy to me to see him so nonplussed as he was,

puzzled to understand how he had missed his effect. That glare of his burnt the smile out of his eyes for an instant. Then:

"Let us hope that you have hardly the experience to speak with authority on that subject," he sneered. He bowed me through the door in silence, and we stood in the salon before he said with his customary air of slightly mocking courtesy, "A glass of wine now and a biscuit before my boy shall drive us back to town?"

But I was determined that he should have no further opportunity to score off me that afternoon. My satisfaction in my small advantage was too short-lived to support my self-control for more than a minute or two, and my endurance was at its limit.

I thanked him for his hospitality, but said that wine was still forbidden me by my medical man and that I feared too much the danger of injury to my shoulder in driving down the hill; and so I took myself off on foot. Save that his carriage passed me and that he was not in it, I have no recollection of my descent of the hill, of whom I met in the streets, or of how I reached my uncle's door. The house I found in that state of festive distraction which generally accompanies the preparations for a feast greater than ordinary. To admit me Barry, in shirt sleeves and green baize apron, left the superintendence of two waiters hired for the occasion, who were laying the long table in the dining room. Miss Felicity, he told me, was giving the final touch to the flowers in the drawing-room with her own hands, and immediately led me thither.

I know that the room must have been filled with light at that hour on such a day. For the house stood high enough, and the sun, sloping to the hilltops beyond the river, flooded it with radiance. But in my memory it remains a place of gloom, Felicity a slim silhouette with a golden nimbus about the head; her new maid, who was assisting her, the smart young girl whom Monsieur de Saint Loup's munificence had substituted for Vashti. Even her voice sounded unreal, her words a patter of amenities.

"Why, Robert, how good of you to come! Though you are wrong to expose yourself to the chill of the twilight, as you will if you stay here more than a moment. Hebe, this work can wait until I call you. Sit down, Cousin Robert."

"Nay," I said heavily. "Let us enjoy the last of the sunshine, Cousin Felicity. Let us walk in the garden till the sun is down. What I have to say will take no longer."

I said no more, nor did she, until the girl had fetched her cloak and we stood on the gravel path whence the great wolf had glared in upon us that night of her arrival, which now seemed so long ago. Then I burst out:

"Felicity, you cannot mean that you will actually go through with this!"

"Can I not?" she broke in before I could say more. "Should I have sent Vashti away — Vashti who brought me up — and old Henry who was my father's little body-servant when they were both small boys, if I were not determined to go through with it?"

Her tone was so sad, so charged with melancholy resolution, that I looked at her as I believe one seldom looks at the person with whom one is speaking, at least when one is young and charged with honest indignation, searchingly and with the will to understand. She met that look with eyes of utter candor, her brow smooth, her lips so lightly firm that there were no lines to mar the beauty of her mouth. And at that look I despaired of changing her. Nevertheless I spoke what I had come to speak, and with hardly a pause after she had ceased.

"The man is vile, Felicity — a sensualist — and cruel. I am just come from spending an hour with him, from seeing the house in which he means you to live with him. I cannot tell you — no young girl would understand, perhaps — "

"I understand enough to know that he is cruel — that I am all the more desirable to him because he knows I loathe him, that I love you. I told him — "

"You told him that — that you loved me!" I cried, my eyes fixed upon the proud poise of her head and the clear glance that went with her avowal.

"Yes. He asked me. I had done what I told you I would do — told him that, if he took me, he would take me unloving. His answer was that I would not be the first who had come to him reluctantly to remain his devoted slave. Later — it was the evening after the one on which I promised to marry him — he asked me if I did not love you and, when I hesitated, reminded me of how he had found us together that twilight in the snow when the wolf wounded you. I said that at least I had thought I loved you then.

" 'You love him yet,' he insisted.

" 'Monsieur,' said I — we were speaking French as he likes me to do with him — 'Monsieur de Saint Loup, since it appears that you wish to hear me say so, I should love Robert Farrier this moment, with all my heart, if I allowed myself to do so.' "

"Felicity! My dear!" I cried. And in another instance I would have caught her to me somehow, my crippled arm in its sling and bandages, notwithstanding. But she stepped quickly back, both hands up, palm outward, to hold me off.

"Don't," she whispered. "No — no — not that I am his. It

might even please him that our love should so betray us. But it would be too sweet, my dear. I could not go on, could not do what I must do, after that."

"Oh, but this is horrible!" I exclaimed. "You must not do it. Go to our uncle, tell him how you feel about this man. Or, if you will not, I will, and add what I know, what I learned this afternoon. It would fill him with horror, the mere thought of your making such a sacrifice. He would drive the villain from his door."

"And die, a ruined and broken old man, before the spring," she added with sad conviction.

"You cannot be sure," I argued. "And if he should, he is already an old man; he has had his life. In ten years, at most, he will probably die. Must your whole life's happiness be sacrificed to buy him ten more years of the affluent self-importance without which he cannot live? My dear, it is wicked — worse than wicked — silly!"

"Robert," she said gently, laying light hands upon the sling that held my right arm, "silly or not, it is what I have to do. You do not know everything that moves me; and, meanly though you think of our uncle, it is much to his credit that he has not told you now, when he must guess something of your opinion of him. I owe him far more than the food and shelter and affection which he has given me. But for him, but for the very large sum which he advanced two years ago, my father would have died in prison — not a debtor's prison, where the most honest man may come through misfortune — but a prison for felons and knaves. Our uncle's money — for no better reason than that his wife's sister had been my father's wife — made good my father's wrongdoing before it was discovered. I found it out in going through my father's letters after his death. Our uncle never told me. To this day he does not know that I know it. I — "

"Perhaps it isn't so then," I broke in. "More likely you misunderstood some transaction. Your own father — is it probable that he — "

She shook her head with a wan smile at my eagerness.

"I thought of that. I took the papers to my father's lawyer. I felt I had to know. So you see," she went on after a deep breath, "if my father's daughter can do anything — even the slightest thing at the greatest sacrifice — to insure the same peaceful ending for her uncle that he gave to her father, she must do it, my dear. Mustn't she? Noblesse oblige." And she gave me a smile with lips that trembled now, and out of eyes shining with unshed tears.

"But, if Uncle Barclay hadn't used that money in that way, it would all be tied up in his business today," I said stubbornly. "It wouldn't help him now."

"But he did use it that way," she replied, and I had no answer for that.

XIII. – THIS MAKES SIX

But now, all at once, I thought I saw a way out in another direction. The idea flashed on me so brilliantly, so like a swiftly widening stream of sunshine when a prison door swings wide, that I did not stop to examine it.

"Look here!" I exclaimed. "Saint Loup has loaned this money – "

"On demand," said she with a little unconscious show of pretty pride in her knowledge of the business phrase. "He can insist on payment at any time until he and Uncle carry through their plan, when the marriage settlement is signed, and he exchanges the notes for a silent partnership."

"On demand, exactly," I exulted. "So much the better. Go ahead and break your engagement. It was no part of the bargain when Saint Loup accepted those notes. Let him demand immediate payment. It will throw the firm into bankruptcy. With times as they are Barclay and Barclay cannot be liquidated by a forced sale of assets at so much as thirty cents on the dollar. How would Monsieur de Saint Loup like losing two-thirds of his money? He wouldn't like it at all. So he'll wait for his money like any sensible man, and even loan more to save what's already in, if necessary. Don't stand there, shaking your head at me. You're not bound in honor. You didn't engage yourself to him on condition that he help our uncle. You – "

"My dear," she stopped me – and God knows it was time, "Monsieur de Saint Loup has offered to release me, if I wished it, saying that he would cheerfully suffer the loss which would come to him through our uncle's backruptcy, if I should decide that I could not marry him."

"He said that? The fiend!"

"Oh, I may as well tell you all of it," she went on. "I meant to spare you – Nay, it was only my own poor pride I would have spared, I fear. When I said I could love you if I allowed myself to do it, he asked me – oh, so gently that I thought for a moment he meant to be kind, even he – if I felt that I could not give you up.

" 'You mean that you will release me?' I cried.

" 'My child, you are free of me from this moment,' said he. 'I will get rid of my house and go away.' And then he added, 'As for the loss that may fall upon me in the liquidation of your uncle's affairs, owing to the necessary withdrawal of my support, I shall pocket that with the feeling that it is a small sacrifice to make for your happiness.'

"I will spare us both the recital of what happened after that, when I understood the full meaning of his speech, and he made clear to me what you have just told me, and I realized that he was willing to lose two-thirds of what he had loaned to our uncle in order to strike back at me. He made me withdraw every word I had said, save only that I loved you. I had, in everything but the actual words, to beg for the restoration of our engagement."

She turned from me as she ceased to speak, and with her head held high, her nostrils quivering, stared across to where beyond the river the summit of the hills looked as if edged with flame from the last rays of the setting sun. The brief warmth of the bright November day was gone in a breath, even from that sheltered spot. In a vagrant gust the green mantle of the ivy shivered on the walls, and the serried shards of glass that topped them glittered like ice in the clear twilight.

"My God," I groaned at last, "that our uncle can be so blind — not to your feelings only, but to the despicable character of this man! Even Vashti — old Henry even — "

She topped me with a dry little laugh.

"Poor Vashti — Did the unhappy creature talk with you? I said what I could to reassure her. But think, Robert, only think what it must mean to entertain an actual belief in such terrors. One must admit that Monsieur was right, cruel as it seemed. Such a maid for his wife would have been intolerable. Oh!"

She ended with a low cry, for De Retz had cleared with easy grace the six-foot, glass-topped wall and alighted almost at her side. He stood, his great head at her elbow, his deep eyes searching her face.

"Go away, De Retz, go away," she commanded. I had never seen her show anything but fondness for the animal; but now, to my astonishment, she recoiled from him, catching my arm and clinging to it, while the hound, his eyes still fixed upon her face, crowded close to her side. "Make him go, Robert. I've come to hate him."

"Be gone," I shouted at the beast and raised my stick. He crouched, snarling, ready to fly at me, as he had always done when I attempted to command him; and the control over my strained nerves, which I had maintained that long afternoon, snapped. The stick I carried had a swordblade sheathed in its shaft. With a pressure of the spring and a single sweep of my uninjured arm I bared the steel and lunged — awkwardly enough, left-handed. But De Retz fled out through the open gate, through the stable yard, to the kitchen garden.

"At least," said Felicity with a shiver, "Monsieur has
90

promised that when we are married he will rid himself of that animal."

It was on my tongue to tell her that even this satisfaction was to be denied her, that Saint Loup was counting on the beast to be his wife's guardian. But to what end, I asked myself. So I said: "But I thought you liked him." For I was still wondering at her new aversion to the hound.

"Not since that night when the wolf attacked you," she told me. "He is so like a wolf. Besides . . . "

"Besides what?" I asked, for she hesitated.

"Oh, it is ridiculous, of course. I must have listened too much to Vashti's foolishness. But of late it is as if De Retz could read my thoughts when he fixes those great eyes on me. Have you noticed that you cannot stare him down as you can an ordinary dog? And his way of sitting, when he is in a room with people, with his forelegs raised from the floor, as if he were trying to assert his equality with them! I asked Monsieur de Saint Loup whether he had ever seen him do it. For De Retz never calls with his master: indeed I have never seen them together. And Monsieur said it was a peculiarity of the breed, both the sitting up and the steadiness of the eyes."

I was numb in mind and will as I walked home through the thickening twilight. My thoughts were but little more than a disordered repetition of the scenes and sensations of the past few minutes: my uncle at the drawing-room window, calling us into the house; his eyes avoiding mine; my knowledge that, even as he spoke his regrets, he was glad that he would not have to endure the silent accusation of my presence at the supper; Felicity's face serenely resolute once more, as it had been when we first went out into the garden; and the firm, cool pressure of her hand at parting.

For a moment I had felt the impulse to take my uncle into his study and tell him of Monsieur de Saint Loup's self-revelation of the afternoon. It was less a reasoned process of thought than some instinctive sense of the uselessness of such a course that prevented my doing so. But as I tramped along and my brain grew clearer, I knew that I had been right. His was not the mind to deal with implications, though these might be none of the subtlest. For him things were what they were supposed to be, and to criticize the quality of a man's passion, so long as it sought its satisfaction in honorable wedlock, would have seemed to him as idle as to criticize his taste for a dinner lawfully bought and paid for.

As for the story of the strip of human skin, its outlandishness would have closed his mind to its significance. Had it been something about a forged check or a cooked

91

account he would have given it his keen examination. But Senegal, pashas, harems and a beautiful Circassian – things he was used to think of as the trappings of an Eastern tale – they would have reduced my story in his eyes to no more than Sinbad or The Forty Thieves.

I could, of course, go to him with the plain statement of Felicity's motives and feelings. I could imagine the shocked dubiety with which he would hear me, his show of lofty unwillingness to believe that any woman, least of all a kinswoman of his, would so traffic with her favors. He would investigate, interrogate her heavily, but not in my presence; and, given her resolution and cleverness and his will to disbelieve, I had little question of the outcome. After that, regarded as a jealous fool by him and by her as a treacherous meddler, all my ability to be of use to her would be gone.

To the one chance by which a way might still open out of all our troubles I gave no thought. With Squire Killian's prolonged absence it seemed to me that my last weak hope in old Peter's will and secret hoard had perished. Even when I reached home and found a note from the lawyer, telling me of his return and bidding me be patient but a little longer, it did not revive. But something more precious had revived in me. This was my courage, which in some strange way seemed to have deserted me since that night when the wolf had mauled my shoulder. It had sprung up with my fury and flourished as De Retz fled from my naked blade. Perhaps in calling it courage I give it too high a name, for it brought me no hope with it. It was only the dogged will to fight on until my fate should be compelled to crush me.

I grew hot with shame as I thought of how I had cowered hitherto. With my right arm ruined I had done nothing – save for a few discouraged attempts at writing – to develop my left. My lunge at the hound in the garden had been ridiculous in its wild impotence. I gritted my teeth with vexation to think that, had I been able to thrust truly, De Retz would now be dead. If I could have known what a coil of villainy would have perished with him, I believe my mortification might have undone me.

I put my new spirit into service at once. At supper I would have none of the assistance which it had become my kindly housekeeper's habit to render me at table. I announced that I would arise, shave myself, and dress before breakfast, though my awkwardness should delay that meal till noon. Then, leaving her bewildered by advice that she should not be alarmed by any unusual sounds, I carried two candles and my father's dueling pistols to the cellar and passed the evening in firing at a mark.

It was slow work, loading and re-loading the weapons with one hand, while my knees gripped them muzzle uppermost. My shooting was execrable at first and improved slowly. But my left hand was being trained, both on the trigger and by the delicate operations of pricking and priming. Best of all, I could feel that I was winning back the powers of a normal man, a man able to hold his own among his fellows. My mind grew busy with plans. I would really apply myself at writing. I would have a quiet horse saddled and brought round on the morrow, with a stable-boy from the tavern to accompany me at first. If Felicity were never to be mine, at least, I told myself, I would no longer submit to be such a poor creature as no girl in her senses could wish to marry. I recalled a line or two of some pompous old play, I forget by whom, and can now remember only an approximation of the words:

It is not given to all men to achieve success;
But we'll do more, Horatio: we'll deserve it.

It may seem strange that in my shooting I had no serious thoughts of a duel with Monsieur de Saint Loup. But my common sense told me that to fight with him would be to risk everything on the outcome. Nevertheless, when the slim bar of the pistol sight wavered here, there and everywhere but on the target, nothing steadied it like his plump and ruddy face as my imagination conjured it up before me. And I could conceive of a state of things that would demand the hazard of such an encounter.

Next morning, strong in my new resolution, I would have put old Goody out of the room the moment she had set down my hot water jug, but she was too full of news. The wolf had been abroad again. While I had been walking home in the twilight, Aggie Van Zile's cur had been slain by it. The unhappy child herself, frightened into fits by the onslaught, had died of her terror a few hours later. At least no other explanation could be made to fit the circumstances. There had been no witnesses of the affair, and Aggie had never been able to give any account of it.

I was still pondering over this, my face smarting from more than one razor cut on cheeks and chin, when I heard her on the stairs again about an hour later. As usual her wheezing utterances heralded her approach, for she always began what she had to say at the bottom of the flight and kept repeating it until she was in my room. But this time I was evidently not the person to whom she was speaking.

"No, sir. No, sir. I was scared enough of what he'd do to himself with his left-handed shaving without having a terrible thing like that to upset him."

"Quite right, too." They were Mr. Sackville's round tones

that answered her. "Bad news always travels fast enough without our helping it forward."

With one end of my neckcloth in my teeth I gave the other a final yank, worried one arm into the sleeve of my father's old wadded dressing gown of plum-color brocade and, pulling it over my wounded shoulder, got to the door in time to open it for them.

"What has happened, sir? What is your bad news?" I asked, forgetting to give the rector so much as good morning. At his words all that was morbid in my imagination had leapt to life. A dozen specters of calamity raced through my mind, and each involved Felicity in a fate more dire than the last.

"Why, Robert!" he cried, and gave my hand a hearty squeeze. "What excellent progress you are making every way!"

"And high time, too," I answered shortly. "I have been making a baby of myself, physically and mentally. Don't try to spare me, sir. What is your dreadful news? My uncle — my cousin?"

"Both of them are in excellent health. You may rest assured as to them — as yet," he added, and then looked for an instance as if he would have dearly loved to recall the last two words. "No. It is poor Killian."

"Killian!" I exclaimed.

"Yes — found dead in his office very early this morning — suicide."

I sat down abruptly on my bed. Those hopes of mine which were based on the lawyer and his efforts to find the missing will and the miser's hoard, and which I had made so great a show of dismissing from my mind — this definite termination of them, added to the shocking news of his death, made me sick and dizzy. Mr. Sackville sent Goody down stairs to fetch me a cup of coffee. Then he said:

"I happened to be the one to find him."

"But he only got back last night," I said idiotically, as if that made the slightest difference.

"You knew he had returned?" the rector took me up. "Not many people did. He didn't come to supper at your uncle's, declined some days ago by post, saying he did not expect to come back in time for it. Did you see him? Have you any idea of the hour — Forgive me, my boy. I am running on like an old woman. But the thing has shaken me, I admit. Squire Killian a suicide! A man of his steadiness, his rectitude, his utter lack of those nervous and imaginative qualities which one associates with self-destruction!"

The story of the rector's dreadful discovery was soon told. On returning a little before midnight from the supper party at my uncle's, he had been summoned at once to attend the deathbed of the little Van Zile girl. There was but little spiritual comfort that he could administer to that wretched household. He remained to the end, however, and it was on his way home in the early hours of the morning that he had spied a light in the lawyer's office. With the thought of burglars, it was characteristic of the gallant old man that he wasted no time in looking for the watch but, gripping his tough ebony staff, tiptoed up the steps and peeped through a chink in the drawn curtains of the window beside the door. The room was well lighted by candles burning on the desk, evidently. But all he could see from where he stood was a section of the floor, the base of the desk and, in the shadows, Killian's legs and feet still in the muddied riding boots in which he had returned.

For a moment he thought of slipping noiselessly away. Then, depressed as he was by the scene which he had just left, it occurred to him that a few minutes' chat would make an agreeable preparation for slumber and he lifted his hand and knocked. He knocked once more and again. The legs in their muddy boots never moved. Had his old friend fallen asleep after his long ride in the wintry air — or was he ill? There was something not altogether like the relaxation of sleep in the posture of those booted legs. Mr. Sackville tried the door. It yielded, and he entered.

Squire Killian was seated bolt upright against the back of his elbow chair, his left hand gripping the edge of the desk, the arm straight and rigid, keeping him so. But his head had fallen toward his right shoulder. A great, gaping gash had ripped open the left side of the neck from beneath the ear almost to the Adam's apple; and in the fingers of the right hand, which rested in his lap, still lay the slim, long-handled penknife which had wrought that ghastly havoc. His shirt, the folds of his loosened stock, the shoulder of his slightly shabby coat, were soaked with blood. There was a pool of it in the shadow of the desk, which Mr. Sackville didn't see until the soles of his shoes slipped and sucked in it. When he came to this part of his narrative he looked down at his now immaculate footgear as if apprehensive that something of that dreadful fluid still adhered to them.

The watch, when he found them, were able to add a little to the knowledge of the circumstances, although nothing toward an explanation of the lawyer's unhappy deed. They had seen him an hour before as he came down the High Street and entered his office. He had "walked pretty wide," they said.

"As if he had been drinking?" the rector asked.

Well, if it had been anybody else, they might have thought so. A constable doesn't willingly own to such a suspicion

95

regarding the attorney to the Town Council that employs him, Mr. Sackville reminded me, especially when they suppose him to have been supping at the house of one of the Councilors.

The French gentleman's wolfhound had been with the lawyer, trotting four or five paces behind him, as a lonely dog will sometimes keep company with an acquaintance of his master's whom he happens on late at night. The animal went right up to the office door with him, and would have gone in, if Squire Killian, turning on his threshold, had not sent him off with a kick and a curse.

"And now," said the rector, when he had finished his story, "will you tell me how you knew Killian had returned? You shall speak in confidence," he went on when I hesitated. "The coroner will not be interested in such a point. It is a clear case of suicide, and he will look for the motive in our poor friend's affairs, though we who knew Killian know that not the smallest irregularity will be found there. The cause lies deeper, in something sudden — some shock so great that his reason shook and he destroyed himself before he could recover from it — or I am much mistaken."

I gave him Killian's note and in answer to his questioning look, when he had read its cryptic phrases, told him the whole story of the missing will, the lawyer's theory about old Peter's green coat, his stubborn belief that with it would be found the solution of the whole mystery, his expectation of finding it somewhere on the miser's former property, and his intention of searching for it on the preceding night, which was what the note had been intended to convey to me.

"You can see how impossible it would be to tell such a tale to the coroner's jury," I ended, but I think he hardly heard me. He was poring over the slip of paper which Killian had written not eighteen hours before, as if to fix the appearance of every word and letter on his mind. Then he rose to his great height and stretched his arms like a man testing his muscles for a task which will take all the strength he can summon to it.

"This makes six, counting man and beast," he said slowly, his light blue eyes on mine: "seven, counting you, my boy. My dog Nero, the only animal that might have matched De Retz, fell first; then Armitage, then Sammy Rogers, poor, crazy Aggie and that wretched cur of hers last night, you crippled, and poor Killian, driven out of his mind, dead by his own hand. Has it occurred to you," he burst out impulsively, "that either old Peter's property has been involved, or Monsieur de Saint Loup's interests and convenience have been furthered, by each of these happenings? Don't attempt to reason with me. I know the thing is moonshine."

"You mean you would hold Saint Loup responsible?" I

asked in amazement.

"If it were not impossible that he should be responsible, I should gravely suspect him," he answered seriously. "He has profited, or stands to profit, by every one of these horrors."

XIV. – THE RECTOR RIDES HIS HOBBY

In our community we had got beyond burying a suicide at a crossroads at midnight, with a stake through his heart, thank God! But, of course, the rector had to deny poor Killian burial in consecrated ground. He had the grave dug on the glebe land, just under the churchyard wall, however; and – brave, charitable soul that he was – he read some prayers over it and in a short oration commended the few of us who followed the coffin from the house. The bishop, should he hear of it, might make of it what he liked.

After all was over he asked me to remain and help him supervise the closing of the grave. He had filled with stones and bowlders as great as two men could lift, until only a few inches of earth were necessary to raise above them the customary sodded mound. No body snatchers or resurrection men should disturb our good friend's rest in that unhallowed spot without more trouble than the task would pay them for.

To avoid the unpleasant consequences of notoriety the burial had taken place in the gray light of the tardy November dawn. But these precautions took so much time that the hour set for Aggie Van Zile's funeral had arrived when they were finished; and although touched by pity for the small rough coffin, the blear-eyed sot of a father and the slattern mother, I remember my bitterness at thinking how lightly the earth might lie above this wretched half-wit, while a useful citizen and honest friend must be crushed under a heap of rocks, because he had flinched from beneath a burden too heavy for him to bear.

What that burden had been the closest examination failed to discover. His own affairs and those of his clients were found to be in the most perfect order. His widow, a small, stout, colorless woman, whose housekeeping and religion absorbed her whole life, could offer no explanation. He had returned from his journey about sunset in excellent spirits. He had indeed pained her by loudly singing a worldly song, little better than a tavern catch, and after supper he had set out for his office, still humming it, telling her not to expect him until very late. That this cheerfulness sprang from the expectation of finding the miser's will and hoard, which was implied in his note to me, seemed more than probable. Mr. Sackville thought so too. But it got us no further forward with that puzzle than with the motive for the lawyer's frantic act. What Killian had known, or guessed, had died with him; and I had neither the authority nor the physical strength and activity to prosecute such a search as in my ignorance it would be necessary to make.

I put the matter behind me again — its promise of wealth, of my uncle's prosperity, Felicity's love and our wedded happiness — as a young man puts behind him his boyish dreams of easy success and quick distinction. As I look back upon the three weeks that followed, I seem to myself to have been like a person under a charm, spellbound by my own determination. I had a single purpose: to put and keep myself in a position to be most helpful to Felicity, and for that end to restore my powers as soon as might be to something like their former strength. It was the difficult and exacting employment of the latter task, no doubt, that made it possible for me to endure the ordeal which from the very outset was entailed by the former. I could not eat a meal, turn the pages of a book or swing a cane as I walked abroad, without being made aware of the challenge of my disability; and the small daily successes, both in recreating the powers of my ruined hand and arm and in circumventing the difficulties of getting on without it, were a constant stimulation to the strange faith I had in the course which I had chosen.

Each morning my toilet required a little less time for its completion; the exercises in left-handed penmanship, with which I occupied myself until the afternoon, became easier and less illegible. Presently I took them with me to the counting-house and found opportunities to be generally useful there. At the same time I judged it safe to dispense with attendance on my afternoon rides. The doctor allowed me to go without my sling; and with the bight of the reins caught about my right wrist I could lengthen and shorten my grip of them at will. Each evening I came up from my cellar with eyes smarting, ears ringing from the smoke and the detonations of my pistols in that confined space, but with the satisfaction of knowing that my arm grew steadier, my hand more dextrous.

I called upon Felicity one afternoon quite early in this period. And then, perhaps more than in any other single instance, my new courage saved me from what might easily have been disaster. Hebe, the maid, answered my knock and told me that Felicity was not at home. I called again the following afternoon to have her tell me the same thing. In the state into which the knowledge of Felicity's engagement had thrown me I should have gone away, too deeply hurt to return, for I had excellent reasons for believing that she was in the house. But as I was, buoyed up by effort and exercise in the frosty air, I had the sense to grow suspicious. There was a

98

suggestion of insolence in her manner, moreover, which I could be certain was no reflect of her mistress's feeling toward me. So I replied with the freedom which my relationship permitted me that I would wait until her return, and I was not greatly astonished when she came into the drawing-room a few minutes later. She did astonish me however, when upon my reply to her reproaches for having neglected her she rose and, moving quietly to the door, pulled it suddenly open. Hebe, who must have been kneeling, ear to keyhole, measured her graceful length at Felicity's feet.

"Fetch Barry to me — Come back with him," Felicity commanded sternly; and when the two servants stood before her: "Barry, give this girl some work that will keep her fully occupied until supper. The flagstones in the scullery want scrubbing, I happened to notice this morning.

"When she complains to her master," Felicity went on after the drawing-room door had shut us in again, "he may understand that I will not tolerate her coming between me and my friends any more than her listening at keyholes."

"Her master?" I exclaimed, stupid and incredulous. "You cannot believe our uncle would set her to such tasks!"

"Our uncle? No, my dear cousin. My intended, Monsieur the ci-devant Comte de Saint Loup, is her master, whatever his pretense of having given her to me. They are his orders which she has been carrying out against you; and she — "

I broke in upon her. There was a bitterness, a cynicism, in her tone which was dreadful to me. But I had no more than my old protests to stop her with, and those she checked at once.

"Robert," she said gently, "you came to give me pleasure, did you not? Then let us speak of pleasant things, the great improvement in your health and strength, for instance. When I took your right hand just now, I thought I could feel a decided pressure of your fingers on mine."

"If that hand will ever close again, it will be to clasp yours," I told her.

As I look back across the years to that unhappy time, we two seem like those Christians of the early persecutions who in their ecstasy caressed the horrid instruments that gave them martyrdom. Hopeless as we were, we still sought meetings which could only give us pain, and shrank not even from those at which we knew that our tormentor would be present. I tacitly reestablished my old custom of supping at my uncle's on Fridays, although Friday was one of Saint Loup's regular evenings for supping there and it gave him, I felt sure, exactly the cruel pleasure he most enjoyed to see us together.

On the very first of these occasions he drew me into the discussion over the date of the wedding, which was still to be set. He urged as early a day in December as the completion of the trousseau would allow. My uncle desired to postpone it until after the tenth of that month, the date of the first of the winter assemblies, which would give him the opportunity of presenting his prospective nephew-in-law to the various notables of the county who had not already met him. Even that put the wedding less than three weeks away. But, although I took my uncle's side, I believe that I contrived to do so without showing that I snatched at any excuse for deferring the fatal event as long as possible. Felicity's quiet announcement that she could not hope to have her things ready before the tenth settled the question. The twelfth was decided upon.

What was more difficult to endure than all this was the sight of the change in our uncle's manners and habits under the influence of the Frenchman's society and the things which his intimacy brought with it. I saw it first in the clouded glance and tremulous hand which he brought to his business of a morning; in the alternation of bland good humor with outbursts of febrile irritation which began to replace that studied equanimity in which he took such pride. At my first appearance at his table since Felicity's engagement I was astonished and alarmed to observe how he, for whom a second glass of port had been a matter for debate with his conscience, now kept a bottle to himself, and emptied it before leading us to rejoin Felicity in the drawing-room. His language and conversation, which had so often bored me in the past by their over-refinement and correctness both in subject matter and expression, amazed me by their freedom; but less so than his tolerance of the rancid jests and perverted allusions with which Saint Loup saw fit to entertain us over our wine. My uncle's were no worse than the roystering indecencies of the taproom, but the Frenchman regaled us with such unnatural and recondite obscenities as were properly graced with the furtive smirk with which he uttered them, and, as often as not, left us two staring in honest yokel-like incomprehension.

Hard with the intolerance of youth and my own special bitterness, it was not until long afterwards that I saw in my uncle's potations his remedy against these outrages and realized that in tipsiness alone could he find a refuge from the assaults of this man whom he dared not check. Only once did he show his disapproval, and that by no more than rising abruptly and stalking from the room. This was upon Saint Loup's asking my opinion of the maid. I answered drily that she would probably prove well enough as soon as Felicity had trained out of her an inclination toward insolence which I had observed.

"Oh, but I did not mean as a servant, mon cher cousin," he laughed, using a form of address which he had lately adopted with me because, I suspect, he saw the effort it cost me not to flinch at it. "I did not mean as a servant, and I think you quite well knew that I did not, you American hypocrite. Would you care to have her? Felicity is not pleased with her. I will sell her to you for what I paid. A charming trifle for a bachelor's establishment — a young Venus — and no tyro, believe me. I should not have got her, save that the young Southern gentleman to whom she belonged ruined himself at cards while on a visit to New York. Should you care to try her, I will send her to your house tonight after her duties about Felicity are over. She shall return here before daylight. No scandal, you see. Even your cousin will not know she has been gone."

He rose punctiliously as my uncle marched past him at this moment. I also had risen and made a step to follow, when he rolled up his eyes and gave me a wink. Doubtless he knew that, though my fist was doubled, it was with the intensity of self-restraint and he had nothing to fear from me.

In Felicity's presence he kept within bounds, seeming to know to the width of a hair the limit which he could not transgress without arousing such indignation as would count any sacrifice cheap for its satisfaction. But he had another form of torment for these times. Knowing how dearly my uncle held his public office, he would twit him on some one of the numerous and obvious shortcomings of the town's administration. Most of all it pleased him to allude to the reward paid for the timber wolf which had been killed so far up in the hills and to dwell upon the slaughter of Aggie Van Zile's cur, which had happened soon after.

Another outrage, which was popularly attributed to the same agency, and which was perpetrated about ten days after Squire Killian's death, gave him a new peg whereon to hang these witticisms. On a certain morning it was discovered that the mound above the lawyer's grave had been destroyed, the earth pawed away and the heap of guardian stones laid bare from end to end. The damage was repaired and a watch set the following night. But next morning a similar desecration was discovered in the churchyard itself. Aggie Van Zile's grave had been dug open to the coffin lid. Indeed it was whispered that the marauding beast had not been stopped by that. At all events, the rector, finding the open grave on his early morning round of the church property, had half filled it in with his own hands before he called the sexton to bring a cartload of stones for its complete protection.

Mr. Sackville came to sup at my uncle's on the third Friday evening on which I also was a guest. The wedding was now less than a week distant, and talk of the arrangements for the ceremony engaged the greater part of the conversation at table. But after Felicity had left us to our wine Saint Loup appeared to see in the clergyman's presence no obstacle to his customary amusement. Recapitulating the circumstances of the payment of the reward and the subsequent depredations attributable only to the beast whose death had been paid for, he called the rector to witness to the justice of his animadversions.

"You, sir, though a man of the cloth and almost entirely unversed in secular affairs, would have known how to manage better, would you not?" he challenged, and sat back in his chair, with his low growl of a chuckle in anticipation of watching the clergyman squirm between falsehood and the admission in his Senior Warden's presence that that gentleman had taken part in a highly foolish proceeding.

But, like all evil men, especially very clever ones, he under-rated the courage and the intelligence of good men. Mr. Sackville did not squirm. He had as little fear of telling my uncle the truth as he had of the poverty in which he might end his days, should my uncle make it impossible for him to go on being rector of St. Michael's. The blue eyes were wintry as he fixed them on that dark and derisive countenance for a moment before he replied.

"Why, as to what I would have done in those circumstances, I do not know," he said at length.

"Oh, come, sir, come. No shilly-shally, I beg," the Frenchman insisted. "We are among gentlemen. Mr. Barclay will not – "

"But I know what I now would do," Mr. Sackville cut short his banter. "Were I their honors the Town Council, I would order the watch to shoot a certain foreign wolfhound on sight and bring its dead body to the council chamber for identification. That is what I would do, sir, and after that I would be much surprised if this community were troubled again by such depredations as have for the last two months disgraced it."

Nobody moved – nobody breathed – for a long moment after that. The full ringing tones in which the clergyman had spoken seemed to continue to sound through the room. Then my uncle, who had been in the act of filling his glass with port for the fourth time, set the bottle down and pushed it from him with a gesture of decision.

I cannot tell how I knew this, for my eyes were fixed on Saint Loup's; and if ever man saw the glare of Hell's own hate in the eyes of another, I saw it leap from his in that long moment of silence. Twice his lips opened and twice closed again before he spoke. Then he said suavely:

"You forget, I think, sir, that my poor De Retz had not arrived until after this series of outrages was well begun."

"Had he not indeed?" Mr. Sackville returned. But all the fire was now gone out of his tone. He smiled with an amiable whimsicality as he went on. "I remember, however, our first conversation, in this house, concerning your hound's name, and how through a misconception of his namesake I associated him with the old werewolf superstition. Has it occurred to you, Monsieur de Saint Loup, that in the Europe of the Middle Ages these recent depredations would have been attributed to such an agency? This desecration of new-made graves would have added the final touch of certitude, would it not?" And with a face beaming with the genial enthusiasm of the antiquary who is a little mad on his subject he leaned across the table in anticipation of the other's reply.

"I also recall that conversation," Saint Loup answered, a smile on his lips, though in his eyes there could be read a kind of uncertainty as to the clergyman's marked and sudden change of manner. Perhaps he decided that the heat with which Mr. Sackville had spoken was owing to no more than a momentary annoyance at being twitted with his dependence upon the good will of my uncle. He interrupted himself with his deep growl of amusement. "I recall, moreover," he went on, "that I answered you somewhat shortly and that I was sorry for it afterwards and would have apologized, had I thought the matter important enough to trespass on your attention with it. Such small, uncomfortable nuances in our intercourse one with another, do you find them as uncomfortable as I do?"

"To any person of fine sensibilities they must be a frequent occasion for regret, sir," the rector replied cordially, adding, "Then I take it, you cannot enlighten me about the werewolf superstition as touching the desecration of graves. I hoped that perhaps one of those old wives' tales heard in childhood might illuminate the question. I apologize to you for again boring you with it, and to you also, sir." He turned to his host.

"Nonsense! No apology necessary," my uncle assured him. "Your encounter with the wolf that same night of which you have been speaking is more than sufficient to excuse your interest in the general subject, were an apology required. You go about armed since then, I trust, when your errands take you out after nightfall."

"Conspicuously so. One of my pistols is generally in my hand."

"So the beast may see it and retreat trembling?" the Frenchman mocked lightly.

"An experienced beast of prey distinguishes between an armed and an unarmed man." put in my uncle.

"A werewolf now," Mr. Sackville began, his eyes kindling with interest, "a werewolf fears so much as a scratch deep enough to draw blood, I have read. And do you know why? Because, if his skin be broken and blood drawn, he changes back instantly into his human form. Even bruises received as a beast show their mark on his human shape. So the sight of a ready weapon must be doubly terrible to him."

"From your conversation," gibed Saint Loup, "I begin to suspect that you carry a morsel of the Host with you on your nocturnal errands."

"That was the infallible protection against all the Powers of Darkness, of course," the rector replied evenly. "But unfortunately for me the Reservation of the Sacrament, as it is termed, is expressly forbidden by the canons of our church. And would a werewolf respect the sacred elements of a Protestant communion?" he added, smiling.

"Werewolves again? Come, come, sir!" My uncle got up from his chair, humorously loud in protest. "You would ride your poor hobby to death among us, if I let you. Meanwhile my niece will have worked herself blind at her embroidery for want of better entertainment."

Monsieur de Saint Loup rose with the alacrity becoming to a lover at the prospect of rejoining his mistress. The rector kept his eyes fixed upon him for a moment or two in what, from their expression, might have been an absent-minded stare. Then he gathered his long legs under him and stood up with a movement of belated decision. If he had been ruminating he had made up his mind on the subject evidently. The Frenchman's right hand had risen to his head, the fingers passing over temple and cheek bone with a slow, exploratory movement, much as a man reminded of a recent bruise or frostbite will feel of the place to assure himself that it is not still tender without knowing that he does so. But it was not until several days later, not until subsequent happenings shed a lurid illumination back upon each detail of the past two months, that I recalled Mr. Sackville's account of the bruised face which Saint Loup had presented on the morning after his return from New York and the story of the accident to his friend's carriage, by which Saint Loup had explained it. Weak as I was, I had felt little interest in the subject, except to wonder why I had not observed the bruises on the Frenchman's face when he came upon Felicity and me in the snowy twilight of old Peter's wood.

XV. – THE TRAGICAL RIDICULOUS

My uncle bowed his guests before him at the dining-room door, and the rector passed through. But Monsieur de Saint Loup insisted on giving my uncle precedence, claiming the concession with a smile as the privilege of prospective relationship. So I, who had stopped to snuff a guttering candle, followed next behind the Frenchman, though at a small interval, as we crossed the hall. The girl Hebe stood at the foot of the stairs, as if passing on some errand; and I saw Saint Loup pause almost on the drawing-room threshold, turn and give her a nod followed by an imperious backward jerk of the head, which was accompanied by an upward cast of the eyes – the whole movement obviously denoting some place at a distance and above us.

Her only reply was a slow drooping of the lids. She turned and began to mount the stairs, her small feet and exquisite ankles showing at every step, her tapering ivory fingers trailing on the balustrade. And for the first time – as will happen to a young man who has had no thought for any woman but one – I realized her exotic beauty. She looked, I thought, more like a lady going to prepare for an assignation than like the haughtiest servant who has just received an order. Saint Loup's gesture, moreover, could indicate nothing else so plainly as his house above the town.

I looked to see whether Felicity had observed this interchange. She might have done so, for she had risen at Mr. Sackville's entrance with my uncle and stood in talk with them just inside the open door. I watched her narrowly for any sign that she had done so, but in vain, unless her begging to be excused from singing that night and her devoting herself as much as possible to Mr. Sackville were to be taken as such. It did not occur to me that the Frenchman might have wished her – and me also – to see this manifestation of a secret understanding between him and the maid of his betrothed.

He now engaged my uncle in one of those discussions of politics, religion and morals, which were called philosophical in those days and which had been popular for a generation and more among gentlemen of education. I lost myself in puzzling over the rector's conduct in the dining room. His attack upon the reputation of Saint Loup's hound had been so sharp as to be little less than an attack upon the man himself; and behind his sudden shift to the air of the enthusiastic antiquary I had sensed a purpose more subtle than the wish to make amends for a mere outburst of anger. He had attempted to draw the Frenchman out, I felt sure, although to what end or with what success I could not imagine. A sharp exclamation from him terminated these musings, and I realized that I had already begun to divide my attention between them and what my uncle and Saint Loup were saying.

"Nay, sir," the latter had objected. "What is a crime in peace time is an act of virtue in war; the villain of our civilization might have ranked as a hero among the Trojans, or today among the Sandwich Islanders. How can you then maintain even an absolute standard of virtue? At least, I think, you must go so far with me as to deny the existence of evil as an active principle in our world."

He had got thus far when the rector's exclamation of dissent interrupted him. But with a deprecatory wave of the hand he continued:

"What you call evil in a man is no more than an absence of that highly variable quality which you call good, as cold is no more than the absence of heat, if we may believe the natural philosophers. Show a so-called bad man the error of his wrong-doing, its practical foolishness, convince him of that, and he becomes a good man at once."

"Does he, indeed?" Mr. Sackville queried ironically. "What of the Count de Sade, a noble, highly intelligent, well educated — and a devil in human form?"

"Oh, not so highly intelligent, or he would not have let them catch him," Saint Loup demurred. "De Sade is a maniac."

"A matter of terminology, no more," the rector retorted. "Not very long ago he would have been said to have sold himself to the Devil. We have, besides, the authority of Holy Writ. The Book of Job tells us how Satan has been going to and fro in the world and walking up and down in it."

"What I cannot understand," broke in the other, "is how you gentlemen of the cloth, perfectly intelligent on other points, can fail to see the dilemma in which you are placed by this question. You deny Dualism, and yet you cannot explain why an all-merciful God permits his creatures to be preyed upon by this evil principle which you insist upon believing in. But I beg you to spare me your comments on the subject." He softened the effect of this speech with a smile of good-natured mischief. "I have questioned so many churchmen about it that the mere sound of the word 'inscrutable' fatigues me. But I will ask you why, with the increase of human knowledge and the waning power of religion to tyrannize over men's minds, we have a complete disappearance of the grosser manifestations of this evil principle. What has become of that hoard of goblins, banshees, witches, your own pet werewolves and what not, that made nighttime so hideous for our forefathers? What living man of any education believes he has seen one of them, or even a ghost?"

106

"I have sometimes considered the subject in that light," Mr. Sackville replied mildly, "and it seems to me possible that, as man is being permitted by means of his intelligence to bend the natural forces to his will through the use of steam, he has by the same means, though without knowing it, been permitted to overcome the supernatural powers of evil.

"And now, my dear child" – he turned to Felicity – "let us talk of something more amusing. The Assembly – do you hear that it will be well attended? I confess that I look forward to my game of whist with some of our remoter neighbors on those occasions with an eagerness perhaps hardly befitting my cloth."

So the conversation ran on comfortably enough for a quarter of an hour or so. Then Felicity arose and begged my uncle and the rest of us to excuse her. A trousseau was a fatiguing task, in spite of all the anticipations it gave rise to, she explained; and the gentle smile with which she spoke was heartbreaking to me, who read the tortured thoughts behind it.

"Good night, Rene," she said to Saint Loup, speaking in French, and with the same smile she held up her face for his kiss. "I trust your sleep will be undisturbed by either natural or supernatural agencies."

He opened the door for her and would have followed her into the hall, I thought, had she not taken hold of the knob on her side and drawn it firmly to. His smile of acquiescence was quite perfect as he turned toward us, but I guessed that it, too, hid something and I rejoiced to think how his passions must be raging behind it, robbed of those sweet freedoms that season an accepted suitor's good-night.

I made my way home through the frosty streets soon after, in no mood for sleep. So, slipping into my father's old dressing gown, I gave a stir to the fire in the room which had been his study and settled down to read for a while. I forget now the name of the book, but it held my interest until the town clock striking midnight aroused me. Then I became aware of a light, sharp tapping on the window-pane. At first I took this for some branch of the leafless woodbine swinging in the wind; I had risen with a yawn, my hand stretched out for my bedroom candle, when it came again, insistently. I tilted the shade of my reading lamp so that the rays could reach the window. Then for a moment I thought my senses had betrayed me.

On that side of the house there was a small, covered platform or piazza, on which the room opened by means of French windows; and at one of these, her face pressed to the glass, stood Felicity. She was dressed as I had seen her in my uncle's drawing-room two hours before, her cloak fallen from one bare shoulder, the dusky gold of her hair glorious in the lamplight, her face pallid, her eyes fixed on mine. When I am dying I shall see their look of desperate confidence, the deep, violet circles beneath them, the tortured lines of her lovely mouth.

I uttered no word, I believe, as I sprang to the window and tore it open. Nor did she speak till long, long after she was on my breast, my one sound arm enfolding her with gentle strength. Not even then did she lift her face from where she had hidden it against my heart, nor did my lips seek hers. For within me a low, clear voice was telling me that, while ere this her will had ruled our lives, now her strength was gone; in this supreme effort which had trampled down the barriers raised round her by the training of her whole life and brought her to my arms, in my house, at that equivocal hour, it was spent; and now it was I who must guide and control, let it cost me what it would. I cannot say that I thought all this. I only held her close, warm and throbbing, and listened while the quiet accents of that inner voice rang in my brain.

Slowly, timidly, with something like the pathetic courage of a child that ventures on some necessary errand into a room full of elders who may not desire her presence, she raised her head at last and looked at me again.

"Then I may stay? You will keep me?"

"I will keep you for ever," I cried, hardly above my breath, and with a lover's and a fool's desire for asseveration added, "though I have to fight the world for you, starve for you."

Her lips, which an instant sooner would have sealed those first words on mine, drew back, quivering, while tears dimmed, though they could not quench the courage in her eyes. Her voice did not falter, but again she was like a child, a frightened child at a school exhibition who speaks bv rote some scrap of prose so faithfully learned by heart that nothing can make her forget it.

"I mean tonight — that you keep me here until just before dawn. Then I can creep home unseen; and I shall belong to you whatever happens; my child shall be yours. I will never have another."

I am an old man who write these lines; and many thousand times, I suppose, I have reviewed that scene, wondering what I ought to have done and, still more, what I would have done, had the power of decision not been taken from me. For there are gifts not to be refused without mortal hurt to the giver; and this was no raw girl kept in ignorance from her cradle to her wedding night, who knew not what it was that she would give. Young though she was, she was a woman who had succeeded to her mother's place as the mistress and protectress of three hundred slaves, their tutelary deity at matings, births and deaths. To many my course will seem to have lain open and clear before me — as sometimes it has seemed to me.

It would have been the true course of young love as the world delights to see it — when the lovers belong to another person's family. And yet I am pleased — and in certain moods a little proud — that I hesitated, that I remembered there is a price at which love itself is too dearly bought, and that I wondered whether the repudiation of our debts of gratitude to our uncle would not prove to be such a price. I seemed to glimpse him tottering through his final years, a wistful nonentity where he had controlled, his presence a reproach that blighted our happiness and soured the cup of our affection.

Meanwhile I had led Felicity to my chair before the hearth, heaped light, hot wood upon the fire and, kneeling, stripped off her little high-heeled slippers and chafed her small icy feet. She said nothing through all this, nor until she had sipped a little from the glass of my father's old Madeira which I sped to fetch from the locked closet in the sideboard. Then, as if she were only repeating aloud words that had been running in her mind unceasingly:

"It would not be cheating him — unless it is cheating to play a game as one's opponent plays it against one. He has no more love for me — real love — than I have for him. Women are his amusement — have always been. His highest praises of me, to my face, are comparisons with the handsomest of his former mistresses. This miserable girl, whom he brought here to guard me against you, is with him tonight.

"Oh, but I am sure of it. I know it for certain," she broke out with animation, mistaking for incredulity the exclamation with which I remembered what had passed between those two in my uncle's hall. "I saw him sign to her after supper tonight in a way that could mean nothing else, and ten minutes after she had put my light out she was out of the house. I watched her go down the carriage drive beneath my window. So you see, my dear — " And suddenly her eyes were alight, her voice golden, her arms, her young breast and bare shoulders yearning towards me as I knelt upright at her side. Another instant and we should have plighted our faith in an embrace which nothing should have severed.

Through the magical stillness of that moment came a heavy thudding and tapping on the board floor of the piazza. The sound of heavy paws beat at a swift trot from the steps that led down to the lawn to the farther end and back, and stopped at the window by which Felicity had entered. Over her flushed shoulder I saw the great head of Saint Loup's wolfhound, held low and thrust forward, framed in the bristling hair of its neck, glaring in upon us through the pane.

"Don't look!" I cried instinctively. But she had turned toward the sound and, to my consternation, sank back into the chair, her hands over her eyes, limp and weeping. At that I must have gone, for the time being, mad. I did the worst thing I could have done, snatched one of my pistols, which lay upon the chimney piece, and fired at the beast point-blank through the glass. Then, as I saw him leap aside and flee, I caught up the other weapon, tore open the window, and fired again. He cleared the hedge in one of those magnificent bounds of his, and I knew that I had missed the second time.

Inwardly cursing myself for a clumsy fool — though the full extent of my folly was yet to be made manifest — I strode back into the study and drew the curtain over the shattered window. Felicity was still weeping silently in her chair.

"It was only that foul beast of Saint Loup's," I assured her, dropping to my knees at her side. "I missed him but at least I have taught him a much needed lesson."

"No — Oh, my dear, no," she whispered between her sobs. "I could not mistake those eyes. They glared at me through our uncle's window the night I came there. I saw them again in old Peter's wood the night you were wounded. De Retz's are a little like them at times, when he is angry, but — "

I should have known better, in any case, then to try to reason with her, hysterical as she was. But now I had other cause for anxiety. From the street came the noise of windows being thrown open; honest householders, aroused by the reports of my pistols, called to one another, inquiring the cause. I ran to the front door and opened it on a crack, the better to estimate the disturbance and its probable consequences.

"The firing seemed to come from Farrier's garden," called a voice which I recognized as young Thompson the grocer's.

"There was a light showing in the side of Farrier's house. It went out when the shots were fired," shrilled old Miss Van Vleck, who missed little that happened in view of the window behind which she lived in a state of chronic invalidism.

But it was what I saw, more than what I heard, that made me understand our predicament. Bolt upright in the street, facing my fate, sat De Retz. As I looked at him, he threw back his great head and uttered a long-drawn howl. I closed the door, at my wit's end what to do. My garden and house would be the center of active and suspicious investigation in less time than I dared to stop to calculate. The watch was bound to arrive, drawn by the sound of my firing. Worse still, I could hear old Goody Hoskins stirring in her quarters above. What story should I tell to those outside, fully dressed as I was and therefore most likely to know more than anybody else of what had occurred? How was I to prevent my correct and pious housekeeper from seeing Felicity?

"Is it rogues, Master Robert? Is it rogues?" Goody called down the upper stairs. "Wait but a minute and I'll fetch the old musket from the closet."

Already the glow of her candle lighted the stairwell. At the tragical ridiculousness of the situation I could have laughed aloud in my bitterness. Then Felicity at my side, her cloak about her, the hood drawn over her head, had caught me by the arm.

"Quick! She must not find me here. I couldn't bear it," she whispered. "The side door and out through the garden to the alley. . . . Ah, that horrible beast! I ought to have known that he would scent my going and track me — that I can never escape him," she ended with a smothered sob, all her swift courage gone, as again the long-drawn howl of the wolfhound echoed through the starlit street.

Dropping my dressing gown where I stood, I pulled on my greatcoat, snatched up my swordcane and led Felicity noiselessly out of the house by the route she had suggested. From the alley we saw the watch clatter up the street, their lanterns swinging, their halberds at the slope. A network of other alleys and stable-yards, such as every schoolboy learns about his native town, let us out at length not fifty yards from my uncle's house, and I had just drawn a long breath of satisfaction at a risky business well accomplished, when with a low cry Felicity shrank against me.

De Retz was at her side, pressing his head against her arm with all that air of satisfaction in his own cleverness which a dog is wont to show when he overhauls his master or mistress unexpectedly. Had I dared, had my task been less imperative, I believe that in my anger I would have flashed out my blade and striven to slay him on the spot. But we were all but under my uncle's windows now. Any disturbance, a cry from the creature if I should fail to kill it instantly, would have brought him out of bed to learn the cause. For it was notorious in the house that he was sleeping badly of late.

"The key," I whispered. "Have it ready. God alone knows when it may enter this beast's head to howl again."

But the hound did not more than trot beside us and wait until Felicity had unlocked the heavy door and vanished into the thick darkness of the hall. He made no move to follow when I went in after her; and, for a long minute, we stood locked in an embrace which was our first as lovers and might well be our last.

111

When she had closed the door upon me and I heard the faint snick of the bolts shot home within, the creature sniffed at the naked shrubs that flanked the steps and, without another glance at me, made its leisurely departure in the direction of the carriage-drive and his quarters on the kitchen porch. I reached home by a circuitous route an hour later to find the neighborhood again in peace, but Goody Hoskins up and voluble with an account of how some passerby must have mistaken the French gentleman's hound for the wolf and fired his pistols at it. One of the bullets had smashed a pane in one of my study windows. As my house stood on a corner, this was a not impossible explanation for outsiders; and the first of old Goody's usual winter colds had kept her from noticing the odor of powder-smoke that must have remained in the air of my study. I humored her by gravely inspecting the damage. But you may be sure that I did not suggest that we search the wall opposite for the place where the bullet had lodged; and she – good, stupid soul – never thought of such a thing.

XVI. – THE ABOMINATION

"He knows all about last night – at least that I was gone and that you brought me home – the rest, too, very likely. I am half ready to believe that he arranged it all beforehand, and that you and I danced on his strings like a pair of marionettes. Hebe had returned: I found her sitting up for me in my room. So he will know all about it if it wasn't a trap which he set for us. And if it wasn't, oh, my dearest – will he not call you out to avenge his injured honor? Run away! Make Uncle Barclay send you on some business errand until the wedding is over and we are gone to New York. Not that I think him a better fighter than you. You may even be the better shot, for all I know, although he boasts of his skill in such affairs. But I dare not risk losing you – dare not face the long years ahead without you. If you love me, go!"

My uncle laid this note on my desk in his counting-room – a little crisp cocked hat of lady's writing paper without seal or superscription.

"Your cousin handed me that for you just as I left the house. I have carried it in my hand the whole way, lest I should forget it. She said it was of the utmost importance," he explained, and stood while I read it, as if by his presence and expectant gaze to draw from me some hint of its contents. He would not read a missive entrusted to him, of course, though it were unsealed; but he would never hesitate to use the compulsion of his personality to learn what it contained, if he could.

"It is of less consequence than she thought, I believe," said

I, and coolly folded up the note and put it into my pocket. "About the account of Roscoe and Son in Chatham, sir — I have been meaning to ask you . . . "

I had not spoken what was not true in saying this. The important thing to Felicity in that note was the danger that Monsieur de Saint Loup might think his honor smirched and challenge me to a duel. But with the reading of her words the certainty that he had indeed set a trap, that we had walked into it open-eyed, and that Felicity had so compromised herself as to be more deeply than ever entangled in his meshes, rolled over me like a wave. Every detail fitted into its place, from his contriving that I alone should be behind him when he gave Hebe that signal in my uncle's hall to the girl's conspicuously surreptitious departure and the loosing of the great hound on Felicity's trail. The beast's behavior had been predictable within narrow limits: its persistent devotion to her had been repeatedly demonstrated. Nor had it needed my insane action with my pistols to frustrate the intrigue which he undoubtedly believed that both of us had plotted. De Retz, banked of his desire to follow her into my house, could be relied upon to howl for admittance: he had done the like when she was paying an afternoon call.

No, Monsieur de Saint Loup would not expose himself to the risk of a duel with me. He would show neither by word nor sign that he was aware of our midnight adventure, but . . . My blood surged into my head at the thought of how he must intend to use his knowledge of that. Let his treatment of Felicity be as cruel as he might choose to make it, with that knowledge he could keep her in his house even after the demand notes which had been his potent weapons hitherto were changed into the comparatively innocuous form of a partnership. With a word of such a thing he could alienate my uncle's sympathy from her; and if she sued him for divorce upon the most complete evidence, he could prove, as proof goes at law, that she did not come into the court with clean hands.

She had written that without me she could not face her life in the years to come. Had she seen what I saw so clearly, that without me to turn to in her need she would have to choose between going on in the yoke of a marriage made intolerable and the disgraceful position of a runaway wife unworthy of the remedy of the law? For without me there would be none to help her, save two old men ill able, the one through his clerical position, the other by reason of defects of character, to be her champion.

Nevertheless I took my pistols with me on my ride that afternoon and got what satisfaction I could out of tying my horse in a secluded ravine and putting ten successive bullets through the ace of spades at thirty paces. And, as I slipped the weapons back into the holsters on my saddle, conscience cried aloud in my mind, "Infirm of purpose! What are you waiting for? When he has possessed her, wearied of her, made her the butt of his malice and his spleen, there will still remain the chance that in a duel he may kill you and not you him." "We will run away. We will hide where he can never find us," I retorted. But the answer seemed so weak, so ignoble, that I had to grind my teeth upon my determination.

I encountered Saint Loup in the High Street as I rode home. Jaunty and dapper, he hailed me with a wave of his tasselled cane and pressed into my hand a tiny box wrapped in jeweler's paper.

"Put that into the pocket of your dress-waistcoat against your standing up with me in church four days hence. 'T is the ring, mon gars, the magic talisman that shall open to me the gates of paradise."

How my hand itched to land flat-heeled across his smiling mouth!

I did not see Felicity alone again, or scarcely at all, until the night of the assembly, the next day but one before her wedding day. God knows how I desired to, how in the long evenings my breast seemed to be no more than one great ache to hold her in my arms again. But when I could endure this no longer and sought my uncle's on some trumped up excuse about the morrow's business, I went in vain. Either a multitude of final touches to her bridal outfit prevented her appearance, or, if I found her, gentle and sedate, presiding over my uncle's coffee or mixing the evening toddy, I found Saint Loup there too; and when I took my speedy departure, it was Barry who showed me out. Wiser than I, and stronger, she spared us both the tormenting sweetness of those hopeless caresses whose lure I could not resist.

So when the night of the assembly came at last, I awaited her coming as a wounded man, for three days thirsting in the desert, awaits the arrival of a caravan which he has sighted far away among the sandhills. For with her as my partner we should be alone together in the heedless crowd; her hand would lie in mine for moments together, her arm press my sleeve; I should breathe the breath of her near presence, and could renew for the last time before she became another's my vow of everlasting devotion.

Swelled by their numbers, the crowd that filled the stately old room, which occupied almost the whole second floor of the town hall, left hardly space for the dancing. It overflowed into the neighboring card room, where at my arrival I saw the rector at his whist. Young men from town and country, whose numbers had not been called for the opening sets, fringed the stair-rail or clustered near the punch bowl by the door, the better to appraise the beauty of late arrivals. These, having cast their wraps below, seemed to float up the stairs like so many goddesses on their clouds of billowy draperies.

From my place in this cordon of polite starers I watched Felicity's ascent on my uncle's arm, Saint Loup at her right elbow. Her heart, I knew, was as heavy as mine, but you could never have guessed it: so lightly did she poise her head; with such gay dignity did she greet the swarm of young fellows who sprang forward to address her or seek an introduction. It gave me a malicious amusement to watch Saint Loup's ruddy cheeks darken as each newcomer in search of a smile thrust him farther and farther behind, and he was compelled to trail along in the cue of her admirers.

Once in the ballroom he made shift to reestablish his position at her side, but only for a moment. Young Philip Dalrymple, whose ancestral estates beyond the river had come down to him from a royal grant and were guaranteed to him by the Treaty of Paris, thrust the Frenchman's short figure aside as if his own six-feet-two of bone and muscle had been unaware of contact with it. Saint Loup turned up to the burly shoulder in blue satin a face suave with readiness to accept the requisite apology. But when none was forthcoming, when Dalrymple in his loud hectoring tones proceeded to monopolize Felicity's attention, I saw the tightened lips, the dull glow that mounted from cheek to brow, the glare that lit the eyes and instantaneously left them leaden as they measured the young bully's size.

"You needn't heed the fellow," I whispered. "He's half tipsy, as usual, and everybody knows it." The which was true. But − God forgive me − my heart leapt at a thought ignoble enough: unless I may claim grace for my extremity.

For, bully though he was, Dalrymple was no coward. The master of five hundred square miles of the northern wilderness, and of a fortune reckoned enormous by our provincial standards, he had left behind him at King's College, whence he had been summarily dismissed three years before my entering there, a legend of harebrained lawlessness and brutality which could have been credible only about one possessed of his magnificent physique and abounding animal spirits. Since then his life had been an alteration of hunting and trapping expeditions − as far as the St Lawrence, it was said − with short, fiery incursions upon the sophisticated viciousness of the capital and the metropolis.

During these forays it was notorious that he was never

wholly sober and never so drunk that he could not think and speak consecutively and point a pistol with deadly aim. He had shot and killed young Van Ryland in a duel under the Jersey palisades, shooting left-handed "for the fun of it," as he boasted. He had sent no less a person than a captain in the Royal Navy back to his ship with a shattered thigh from a duel across the table after thirty-six hours of punch and cards in a private room in Fraunce's Tavern.

As I listened to his talk and watched him preening himself with the vanity which is ever the overmastering passion of such human animals, I judged that Monsieur de Saint Loup would receive scant consideration, should he choose to demand an apology for the rudeness of which he had been a victim. If ever the will for impish deviltry lighted a man's eyes, it gleamed in Philip Dalrymple's.

"Engaged to be married already — to be married the day after tomorrow?" he was chaffing noisly. "Come, come! This must be looked into. In our capacity of over-lord of the middle river we cannot permit the disposal of so much beauty without our personal investigation. In fact it was the rumor of some such thing brought us here. Our taste runs to more highly spiced amusements than country assemblies as a rule. Does it not, Jenkins?" He appealed to a weedy, middle-aged man at his side, whom I now placed as the familiar companion and lick-spittle who figured in most of the gossip about him. "Who, pray, has had the temerity to appropriate all this loveliness to himself without so much as a by-your-leave to me?"

"Permit me, Mr. Dalrymple," my uncle, who had been so far ignored by him, and whose face had been growing more and more austere as the insolent monologue ran on, now interrupted severely. "Permit me to present you to my niece's intended, Monsieur le Comte de Saint Loup — Mr. Dalrymple."

"Monsieur le Comte — ravished by the honor, 'pon my word!" Dalrymple's bow was a masterpiece of polished irony. The fellow had breeding and could show it when he cared to. "It is a privilege to meet any gentleman who, having been chucked neck-and-crop out of his own country, knows so well how to avail himself of the best things afforded by the country of his exile. Pray, how is it done?"

Monsieur de Saint Loup turned to me before replying.

"My dear Robert, will you have the goodness to substitute for me with your cousin?" he added smoothly; and to Felicity, "My dear, I am desolated, but this gentleman has asked me a question which demands an immediate and detailed answer."

We were late; the music struck up as we took our places;

and with my thoughts whirling with the possibilities of this new complication in our fate I had to fix my mind on the well-learned intricacies of the dance, lest I make a blunder. I dared not give Felicity so much as a word about the tense scene we had just quitted, and she was in no better case. Even in the intervals when the other couples bore their part we spoke only of the music, the excellence of the floor, the sudden change of weather from ringing frost to fog and drizzle.

The dance ended and, a part of the elaborately casual little procession of lovers that sought the staircase, we had left the ball room when she pressed suddenly against my arm.

"Oh, Robert, we must not — we dare not — " she whispered. "It must be wicked to wish for the death of anyone. But only think — if they should fight — if he should be — It would mean life again for you and me — and not for us only. An end of this silken persecution for our uncle — "

"My darling," I whispered back, "it may happen. Let his second lose the toss, and Saint Loup will be at Dalrymple's disposal; and that bully is without mercy."

"Oh, Robert, is it wrong to wish it? I cannot help it. I must pay so much — so long! I had steeled myself to endure it. But now that this chance of escape has appeared, it seems to me that, if it fail, my courage will fail too." She was clinging to my arm with both hands now, her face so eloquently uplifted that an old gentleman in the card-room doorway considerately turned his back.

"Even a severe wound may save us." I strove to steady her and at the same time to keep my own head by trying to think rationally. "By the time Saint Loup has recovered from a broken shoulder or a bullet through the body business may have mended so much that our uncle can pay him off, find credit elsewhere."

"Ah, do you think so? But a broken shoulder!" She shuddered so that my anger flamed against this subtle wretch for all the pain he cost her.

"I pray to God," I muttered hotly, "that Dalrymple will kill him. If he does not, the wretch shall fight me, let the risk be what it will."

But she went half wild at that, her fingers twisting in the ruffle on my breast, the warm breath of her protests in my face, so that I had to take her hand to draw it down and lead her forward a step or two, lest we should be remarked even by the self-centered couples who shared with us the open privacy of that place. And it was so, with one of her arms wreathed in mine and her body on tiptoe almost touching my breast, that Saint Loup came upon us.

He was smiling — when we looked up to find him there — much the same smile he had worn when he found my wounded body on her knees that twilight in old Peter's wood.

"Forgive my intrusion, I beg," he began after the smallest pause in which his glance played over us in amused appraisal; "but I have been unable to avoid an affair with Mr. Dalrymple. We are to meet at daybreak, I believe. Robert, mon cher cousin, will you be good enough to wait on Mr. Jenkins and arrange the details? Felicity, my love, will you not honor me with this dance? I feel quite sure that your anxiety for the morrow's outcome cannot have put you out of the mood for dancing."

"Then you little know the strength of my anxiety, Monsieur," she flashed at him with irony equal to his own.

"Look here, sir!" I burst out, as he drew her limp arm through his. "You honor me with a responsibility which I cannot accept."

"Because you earnestly hope young Dalrymple's bullet may find my heart tomorrow morning? My dear boy, that hope is my security, though you were capable of hating me as much as you think you do. I even leave it to you to choose my other second. We know that conscience of his, do we not, my love?" And with a laugh and a playful pat on Felicity's wrist he led her away as the first deep chords of the 'cello summoned the dancers to their places.

It was a couple of hours past midnight, the party was breaking up, before I had the opportunity of speaking with him again. Meanwhile I had found a young lieutenant of Dragoons to assist me. With Jenkins and another of his sort we had agreed upon the details — pistols at twenty paces, on the river bank a mile above the town at daybreak — and managed our conference so casually that not even my uncle was aware that anything untoward was in the wind. He led Felicity to his carriage with that assumption of stately urbanity which was like the breath of his nostrils to him, and Saint Loup bowed over her hand with a confident assurance that he would wait upon her the following evening, if she would permit it.

"We have little more than three hours before we must be astir again, my dear Robert," Saint Loup said briskly as the carriage drove away. "Will you not spend it with me at my house? I must change to a less conspicuous costume, but you need not. And I can promise you a bottle or two of prime Burgundy to while away the interval. It is a long climb up tonight, but I have sent word to my man to have my chaise waiting to bring us down at half-past six."

I was in a mood to accept any invitation that would save me from spending those hours alone in my house, which now, and for ever in my lifetime, would be haunted by the presence of her who had so pitifully and so vainly sought refuge there. So I assented promptly. But, as we plodded up the long hill side by side through the thick mist and drizzling rain, I wondered whether principal and second had ever sat out the hours before a duel with such feelings between them as my hate and fear of him and his cruelty and hate of me; and, if they had done so, whether they could have showed them as little as we did.

His smiling malice and cynical contempt were cloaked by a courteous hospitality which I accepted with every sign of taking it at its face value. We drew our chairs side by side in front of the blazing hearth. Our glasses clinked before the first sip of the wine that brimmed them. We had one plate in common for our cheese and bread; and when he excused himself to change his broad white ruffles and claret colored coat for a high-buttoned black surtout which would present a less easy mark, he urged me to take some rest and brought me a rug in which to wrap myself, explaining that he had some papers he desired to put in order and that he might be occupied for an hour or more.

What with my fears, and my more awful hopes — for it is a most horrid thing to be a man's second in an encounter in which you hope he will be killed — it seemed absurd that I might sleep: above all in that place of silken luxury which only a few weeks back I had seen as the abode of avarice and squalor. It seemed impossible that behind yonder door with its garlanded panels old Peter's tattered throat had stained the deal table with its languid ooze of blood; that in this very room poor Killian and I had pried through the dark clutter of piled-up crates and bales to come upon that naked footprint where now the brazen fender and delicate andirons glinted and gleamed to the blaze. But the fire and the wine warmed and lulled me without and within. The clock in its little, glazed and gilded temple ticked with a swift and soothing iteration like a trickle from the stream of time itself. Now and then, at first, came a slight sound from that barracks-like room which Saint Loup had showed me as peculiarly his own. The drip and murmur of the rain outside mingled with the low flutter and hiss of the burning sticks before me. My thoughts took one fantastic turn and then another. . . .

Ping — ping — ping! It was the soft, silver bell of the little clock, striking the hour. One — two — three, I counted. But it had been long past three — nearly four — when Saint Loup left me. The puzzle brought me wide awake. The burnt-out candles smoked in their sockets; the fire was a heap of ashes; the room was filled with a chill, gray light that crept in round the drawn curtains and showed me the clock's face. The hour was seven. I must have heard only the last three strokes. Already we were half an hour late for our appointment. Had Saint Loup gone without me? I ran to his door and knocked, knocked again and entered. No candle burned there; nor had any been lighted, to judge by the one that stood in the candlestick. But between the open curtains came light enough. The bed had not been slept in; on the writing desk lay pens and paper in the neat order in which his housekeeper had left them.

Had he fled? Was the man a coward at heart, who, finding himself committed to a quarrel with a dangerous duelist, had lacked the courage to carry it through? With a wild thrill of hope I glanced round the room for any sign of preparation for a hasty flight. There was none. Numerous garments hung undisturbed in the armoire. Whips, holsters, pistols, his sword in its chaste elegance of ivory and silver, were all upon the rack where I had last seen them. Only that grisly trophy from Africa, that dreadful strip of the skin of the Circassian odalisque, seemed to have been put elsewhere. At all events, I did not see it, and I drew a breath of relief. For its thin, grayish-white delicacy had haunted me since that day when Saint Loup had put it into my hands.

Swiftly I traversed the small remainder of the house, glanced in upon the scented stillness of the bridal chamber, the scrubbed and polished bareness of the kitchen. Perhaps an unconscious memory of the circumstances in which I had last seen that room by the light of a dripping dawn was responsible for my next thought. Suppose Saint Loup had heard some noise about the garden and stepped out like old Peter to meet a similar fate! The door was on the latch, bolts and heavy bar withdrawn. I tore it open. I can hear now the drip of the eaves, the steady beating of the rain. I can see the small, straight rods of it against the hollows of the wood beyond the ruined wall. Not a breath of wind deranged its vertical lines or shook the crystal drops which beaded every stalk and leafless stem that bordered the garden paths. I can hear and see these things now, I say; so I must have heard and seen them then. But I cannot remember that I did. As I remember it, my eyes fell upon just one thing — the imprint of a naked foot in the sodden clay of the path below me.

Slender, high-arched, delicate enough for a woman's and almost as small, it was the counterpart of the one which had startled Killian and me so many weeks ago in the ashes of the hearth I had just quitted. It pointed away from the house. But before I could rally my senses to look for others like it in the gleaming surface of the path, a sound startled me. Like a low growl it came from the end of the garden. My first thought

120

being of the wolf, I had whipped inside and closed the door to
a crack, through which I stood peering, when I remembered
that Saint Loup had rehabilitated one of the small outhouses
near the breach in the wall, so that his great hound might sleep
there if it wearied of its place on my uncle's back porch, as it
sometimes seemed to do. Doubtless De Retz had heard me
come out of the house and was stirring to investigate, thought
I, though there had been neither anger nor alarm, but rather a
note of satisfaction, in the sound I had heard. In another
moment I would have had the door open again and would have
been standing plainly visible; but something moved at the far
end of the path and kept me where I was.

The stems of the thickly-growing raspberry bushes shook as
if De Retz were indeed pressing through them. But the
hound's thick coat, let it gleam with moisture all it might,
could never have reflected that pale sheen among the withered
stems. The bushes parted, and Monsieur de Saint Loup glided
into the path — Monsieur de Saint Loup stark naked, save for
what looked at that distance like a strip of light gray rag about
his waist. He stopped, his arms hanging from his shoulders, so
that his hands all but touched the ground. Between them you
saw the slack curve of his small round belly as it swung to the
curious trotting movement of his feet. He paused in his
advance at every two or three yards and, with his back held
nearly horizontal, threw up his head with a movement purely
animal and sniffed the still air and listened. I can no more
describe the expression of his face than I can forget it: the
intelligence that informed the bestial satisfaction of the eyes,
the flaring nostrils, the slavering mouth, out of whose vivid
redness shone the long canines.

XVII. – MICHAEL . . . AGAINST THE DRAGON

What I did next had no more of thought in it than the
instinctive recoil of a man who, pushing through dense
thickets, comes unawares upon a pit of filth or a mass of
buzzing carrion. I closed the door; noiseless and swift I
regained the little salon, caught up my greatcoat and hat, and
let myself out into the little porch in front. The post-chaise
stood at the gate, the postilion humped in the saddle beneath
his dripping hat. I may have spoken to him, told him his
master would be ready soon, or some such thing. I do not
know. A sense of outrage possessed me, transcending the
power of conscious thought. Through my mind that
crouching, naked form between the raspberry bushes drew a
long train of half-guessed abominations. Whispered scraps of
the tales of travelers in the high Andes and the Orient echoed
in my ears, and the Mosaic thunders of Leviticus against

similar enormities.

> He shall surely be put to death,
> and ye shall slay the beast.

For, pushed to the very frontier of surmise, so only could I interpret what I had seen.

Where the steep road makes one of its sharpest turnings as it winds downward from Gallows Hill I concealed myself behind the low wall, placed my pistols in a niche between two stones, my handkerchief wrapped round them to preserve the priming from the damp, and waited for the sound of wheels or feet. For there, where Saint Loup must come straight towards me for a dozen yards, I could not miss him. Let him choose to drive, the vehicle must slow almost to a stop in that steep bend, and I would rise up and kill him through his carriage window.

I was quite cool. At least I was without any sense of agitation, and I felt none of guilt. In my own eyes I was the executioner chosen of Providence to rid the earth of one who had placed himself so far outside of law and custom that only by going outside of law and custom could he be punished. I made no plan to escape the consequences of my deed. I saw clearly that even to palliate my guilt I would have to make against my victim an accusation so vile that Felicity — for no stronger reason than her engagement to him — would be followed by filthy whisperings for years to come. But it did not concern me that, lacking such palliation, I should be sent to my death, a murderer and a coward in the eyes of men, a disappointed lover who had lacked the courage to face his rival in fair field.

Some children clattered past my hiding place on their way to school. Saint Loup's post chaise galvanized me into abortive action by rolling down the hill — empty. After that nobody appeared to have occasion to use that road on such a rainy morning. For perhaps an hour I crouched there, unconscious of the moisture that soaked my garments, my body growing slowly as numb as my mind, which was fixed, like it, upon the single thing I meant to do. A sound of footsteps on the streaming ledges aroused me so suddenly that I sprang up, pistol in hand, without waiting to note the direction from which they came. The round tones of Mr. Sackville's voice hailed me from just below.

"Bob Farrier! I've been searching for you. What. . . . ?"

And at the words something seemed to break in my breast, and I reeled, catching with my maimed hand at the stones in front of me for support. He made a half-dozen running steps, laid his hand on top of the wall and landed lightly at my side.

"My poor boy! We haven't come to assassination yet."

With gentle decisiveness he took the pistol out of my hand, picked up the other, and dropped them both into the pockets of his cloak, while I could only stand, biting my lips and swallowing down the sobs that crowded to my throat. Without the power to resist I let him lead me down the hill and by an over-grown path to his back garden gate. He flung his arm across my shoulders at the start, and I caught his hand with my sound one and kept it there, as a child, awakened from a nightmare, clings to the hand of its nurse.

In his study, with the door locked upon us, he poured me out a stiff drink of brandy and stood over me while I choked it down. Then, silent, blowing great clouds of tobacco smoke between us, he sat until at length I lifted my head from between my hands.

"You knew Dalrymple was dead, I suppose," he remarked in a casual tone; and in response to my exclamation of shocked incredulity, "Yes — killed this morning at daylight as he left the tavern to go to his meeting with Saint Loup."

"But how?"

"The great wolf — leapt on him and tore his throat out in a single movement, Jenkins says, and was gone before anyone could raise a hand."

"Jenkins saw it?"

"He and that other under-strapper of the unhappy young man. They were immediately behind Dalrymple as they went out of the gate of the stable yard. Dalrymple's reeling back upon them was their first intimation of the attack. They had a moment's glimpse of the creature on Dalrymple's chest, its fangs buried in his throat. Then it was away and lost in the morning twilight."

"So nobody was at the meeting-place," I exclaimed, speaking the thought that happened to come uppermost as he paused.

"Only your young military colleague. He waited three-quarters of an hour there in the rain, decided it was an elaborate hoax and stormed back to town, uncertain whether to send his cartel to you, Saint Loup, Dalrymple, Jenkins, or all four of you at once. Where were you and Saint Loup, by the way?"

His tone was casual as before, but I saw his eyes narrow as he put the question. In answer I poured out the story of the night. I told it at length. For with every word the intolerable burden that lay upon my spirit grew lighter. Only once did he check me. This was when I mentioned what I had taken for a dirty rag about the Frenchman's naked middle.

"Could that have been a strip of skin? Have you ever chanced to see a piece of tanned human skin?"

So I told him the story of that strip of skin in Saint Loup's bedroom as Saint Loup had told it to me, and of my missing it from its place on the rack there that morning.

"And you have never told your uncle of it? . . . Well, yes. Very likely so," he admitted, relaxing his sternness, when I had explained my reasons for keeping silence. "And that is why you preferred murder to going to him this morning?"

"I suppose so. I don't know the thoughts that drove me to what I would have done this morning."

"I do," he cried heartily, rising and clapping me on the shoulder. "It was your honest goodness in instinctive revolt against this man who is the quintessence of evil.

"Robert," he went on solemnly, standing before me and fixing me with his keen blue eyes, "can you believe? Or have you lost the faculty of belief, like so many in this age who would reject everything which man cannot account for by that creaking contrivance he calls his reason? Have you the power of faith, even faith in a wretched fallible erring creature like me? You believe in a good God, I know — or you think you do. But have you joined the contemporary crowd of ostriches that croak from the sand they have thrust their heads into that the Devil is dead?"

He checked himself abruptly and went on in a more quiet tone:

"Tell me, my dear boy: after the wolf attacked you and you lay for so long before you began to improve, what did you dream of in your delirious state? What did your mind run upon?"

"Good God, sir, human blood!" I cried, shuddering at the memory I had striven to keep far from me. "The blood of children most of all. I loathed it and longed for it at once. And because I loathed it I seemed to long for it the more."

"And these dreams, this longing, merely subsided gradually?"

"It stopped abruptly. You may smile, sir; but it was as if it were charmed away by some hocus-pocus that Vashti performed over me one night when she relieved old Goody Hoskins as my nurse."

"So that accounts for it," he nodded gravely.

"Accounts for what?"

"For your being still in possession of your own soul, and not the bond-slave of the Devil. I suspected — Nay. I did not. But because I have amused myself by studying these things I had put one fact with another, building up a fantastic hypothetical fabric which seemed to fall to the ground when

124

you were able to take the sacrament into your mouth that day in your sickroom. According to the ancient belief in diabolism the consecrated bread would have burned you like a live coal, had I been right.

"Now look here." He unlocked the drawer and took from it a sheet of foolscap which he placed in my hands. "You recognize the writing?"

"Squire Killian's?" I questioned. But I had no doubt of that crabbed script with the humorous little final quirks and initial flourishes. Written in the highest state of excitement as it must have been, the characteristics were unmistakable. It ran:

"After what I have seen tonight I respectfully decline, O God, to remain longer in a world where such things can happen."

"That lay on Killian's desk, the ink hardly dry, when I found him that night dead in his chair," Mr. Sackville explained in answer to my look. "I did not see that it was necessary to the coroner, so I suppressed it."

"You think he had seen — what I saw this morning?" I asked in perplexity. "Surely he wasn't the man to — "

"I think that either he saw more, or understood what he saw as you have not understood it. I believe that he saw Saint Loup change from the shape of De Retz into his proper shape as a man. Oh, consider, Robert," Mr. Sackville cried imploringly: "try to forget for a while our modern notion that, because a thing hasn't been known to occur for a century or two, it cannot occur, and even that it never has occurred. Remember: none of these outrages took place before this Frenchman arrived here. There were none between his temporary departure and the arrival of his hound. Then they recommenced almost at once. And nobody saw Saint Loup's return. No one has seen him and his hound together. They have never been visible at the same time. Saint Loup has never been at his house when I have known that De Retz was hanging about your uncle's or out for a walk with Felicity. No beasts or cattle have been slain hereabouts, no people have been attacked, save those who blocked his way or excited his anger. And of those who interfered with him all have been victims of the wolf, except poor Killian, who was blasted by some portent, and your young cousin's two servants, who appear to have had such means of protection that he had to turn their own poor charms against them by accusing them to your uncle.

"Consider what graves have been desecrated: little Aggie's, whose weak mind knew him at once for what he was; Killian's, who drove him — I believe — to the revelation of his diabolical power. This which you have just now told me of your delirious

125

dreams and Vashti's incantation supplies the only link that appeared to be wanting. Or don't you know that in the old days it was well understood that one bitten by a werewolf turned werewolf himself? If I still could doubt — What do I say? So infected am I by the skepticism of our age that even I feel that I still ought to doubt. But such a belt of human skin as you have seen round my body has been, time out of mind, the apparatus by means of which the lycanthropist has changed to his bestial form."

More than once, and more than twice, I would have broken in on this passionate exposition, if I could. But each time he had kept me silent with a gesture of his hand, and each time a moment more of thought had disposed of my objections. Saint Loup's account of his return from New York in the carriage of his friend rested on nothing but his own word. The letters from him which had come before that return and after the arrival of De Retz could easily have been written before he had himself shipped from New York in his canine form. Any tavern keeper might have posted them for him afterwards. As for the bruises on his face, which he accounted for by an accident to that carriage — I should never forget how Felicity had stood her ground in the snowy twilight of old Peter's wood and broken the hold of the wolf upon my shoulder with blows of my loaded stick. And when I had flashed the blade from my swordcane that afternoon in my uncle's garden, De Retz had fled before my clumsy lunge. Could that have been because a scratch would have revealed him to us, naked and horrible in human form?

"Even if all this could be true," I began.

"It is true," he interrupted me in a low voice.

"Nevertheless can you imagine yourself going to my uncle with it?"

"I can imagine myself going to Monsieur de Saint Loup with it," he said grimly. "You did not fear the gallows an hour ago. I do not fear it now."

As he towered above me, his blue eyes blazing, his hair a silver nimbus about his head, he was like the Archangel Michael in the east window of his old church, and the words emblazoned under it rang through my head like a trumpet-call:

There was war in Heaven. Michael and his angels fought against the dragon; and the dragon fought and his angels and prevailed not.

Since I was a child I had read them on many a Sunday morning.

"Then I go with you," I cried, springing up.

"I knew you would," he beamed upon me. "And we will do well to make haste. We cannot tell what the miscreant will do; but I know that, finding you gone, he will guess that you saw him slinking through the bushes and that you have run with your discovery either to your uncle or to me."

He had turned to take up his cloak, when a knock sounded on the study door, and my uncle's voice followed it:

"Sackville, are you there? Are my niece and Saint Loup with you? I've been waiting in the church for half an hour. Why the delay?"

In two strides the rector had reached the door and flung it open.

"Waiting in the church? What for?"

"For the wedding, of course. Don't tell me they haven't come yet!" my uncle complained, fuming into the room as a man will when he has forsaken important business to keep an engagement and finds that those with whom he has made it have not yet arrived.

"Wedding?" Mr. Sackville asked in amazement.

"Certainly. I gathered from Saint Loup that he had arranged everything with you. He has been called to New York by pressing affairs. He cannot tell when he will be able to return. He came to me an hour ago, begging for an immediate marriage. I gave him a note to Felicity, asking her to consent and to go with him to the church. We were to meet there in a half-hour's time. It is most annoying. I left matters of great importance. I suppose the child is still packing her gewgaws and fal-lals."

"You gave him a note requesting her to go with him?" Mr. Sackville asked slowly.

"To meet me here at the church," my uncle returned, in arms at once against the criticism latent in the other's tone. "Surely, with her affianced husband, a man of honor — "

"A man of Belial, sir!" thundered the rector. "Robert, run round to your uncle's house and see. And when you have seen — for I know what you will find — order your uncle's carriage instantly. Bid Barry drive it, and return here in it for us."

He had handed me my pistols while he was speaking, and dropped on the table two gleaming, heavy slugs.

"Load with those while you are waiting for the carriage," he commanded. "I would give you a morsel of the sacrament for your breast pocket if I could. But there is nothing in the Thirty-Nine Articles against silver bullets, at all events."

So great was the energy, so imposing the conviction, with which he spoke, that my uncle had been able to do no more than stand and stare at him. But now, enveloping himself in the mantle of his dignity:

"You may go, Robert," he said, "since it will oblige Mr. Sackville. You will, however, find Monsieur de Saint Loup's post-chaise at my door, if indeed you do not meet it on its way hither. Anything else is unthinkable."

"Saint Loup's chaise is this moment splashing furiously toward New York," Mr. Sackville retorted. "Oh, my dear old friend, you must listen to me now. This Frenchman — You have ignored my hints, silenced me when I would have told you what I have gathered concerning him. You shall hear me now, though it may be too late."

I stayed for no more, but went hot-foot. I found matters at my uncle's as the rector had foretold. The chaise, with Saint Loup and Felicity inside and Felicity's luggage behind, the maid in the rumble, had driven away in the direction of the church almost an hour before. While I was waiting I drew the old charges from my pistols and reloaded them. It was a relief to have that outlet for my impatience and anxiety; but I felt as if I must be in a nightmare as I hammered home those silver slugs,

Only Mr. Sackville hurried down the path when, half an hour after my departure from the rectory, Barry halted the carriage before the gate. My uncle leaned, white-faced, the mere deflated sack of his usual pompous presence, against one of the pillars of the little white portico. He flapped one large white-ruffled hand at me, and I saw his lips move for a moment or two before I caught any sound. Then:

"Kill him, Robert. Shoot the villain down like a dog," he croaked. "You shall be exculpated. I will see to that."

"May God forgive me," murmured the rector when he had given Barry his instructions and sunk down on the cushions beside me as the carriage lurched forward. "I am afraid I vented my own fear and anger on that poor old man. He forced me to it. He all but forbade any pursuit, harping on that scoundrel's honor, inventing explanations, excuses. But I might have carried conviction by more gentle means, I suppose," he added regretfully.

"You mean you actually made my uncle believe — what you believe?" I asked, incredulous.

"I made him believe as much as his mind is capable of believing — that unless we overtake them his niece will be that villain's trull by tomorrow morning and sold to some woman-dealer when he is sated of her. I told him, too, that worse might happen to her, and so saved myself from lying."

"What could be worse?" I cried.

"A number of things, each as dreadful as the other," he answered gravely. "Such monsters as he is have dealt with their victims in a variety of ways.

"And we pursue him at a foot-pace in this lumbering ark!"
I cried. "We should be riding the swiftest horses to be got in
town. With his light chaise and those fine beasts of his we
should not catch him before nightfall even then. As it is – "

My hand went out to pull the cord for Barry to stop and
turn, but he checked me.

"I am sorry," he said gently, "but, hale and hearty as I am
for my seventy years, I could not endure a long day in the
saddle."

"But I, at least – "

"Forgive me, but let me speak with the knowledge that all
my years of reading about these old mysteries have endowed
me with. Should you overtake him by yourself, you might well
be helpless. The wiles of these creatures of Satan are infinite."

"But we must be falling farther and farther behind them at
every step," I protested.

Indeed, now that we were clear of the town and could feel
the unchecked force of the downpour upon the open country,
our task seemed a hopeless one.

"What is to prevent his taking a boat tonight and drifting
down river with the current? He could be in New York by
morning," I exclaimed bitterly.

"There is nothing to prevent that. But if he changes, so
shall we. Everywhere we will make the strictest inquiries, and
it should not be difficult to trace a vehicle such as his. There
will be few of any sort on the road on a day like this."

I hardly heard him. Through the streaming glass of the
carriage door I saw the stile over which Saint Loup and I had
climbed that lovely autumn day so few weeks back and seen
Felicity leaning from her carriage window to ask us if it were
indeed her destination that appeared ahead. I covered my face
to shut out the memory. Mr. Sackville said nothing more. But
I heard and felt him stirring about, and presently his hearty
tones exhorted me:

"Come, Robert. There is a just God that rules this world,
turning even the successes of the wicked to his glory. Believe
that, and nothing can hurt us. His floods" – he pointed to the
swirling surface of a brook that lapped the planking of the
bridge over which we were rumbling – "His floods may wash
out a bridge or bring down a landslide across the road in front
of Monsieur de Saint Loup. 'In quietness and confidence shall
be our strength.' Meanwhile, unless I am much mistaken, you
have eaten nothing since last night. Here is food. Fall to,
though the first mouthfuls choke you, and you will find your
courage return. Man does not live by bread alone, nor only by
the things of the spirit, though it has always been the weakness
of the churches that they can never bear in mind at once both

sides of his two-fold nature."

He had a cold fowl and bread and cheese set out on a napkin on the seat facing us, and two bottles of the sound dry wine of his own grapes; and when I had done full justice to them, as after some difficulty I succeeded in doing, courage and hope alike revived in me. Exhausted as I was in body and mind, I even slept for a while. It was late afternoon when his hand on my knee awoke me.

"Your pistols," he said quietly. "Our friend ought not to be far off now."

XVIII. — SILVER BULLETS

Ahead, where he pointed over the lowered glass, a post-chaise was down in the ditch with a broken axle, and — Was our mission accomplished? Pacing up and down beside the wrecked vehicle was the slender figure of a girl — Felicity, unless there could be such another fur-trimmed blue pelisse on the road that drenching afternoon.

The roofs and chimneys of a village showed a couple of furlongs ahead. Thither the postilion had gone with the horses to get help, I guessed, since they were nowhere to be seen. But could Saint Loup have gone with him, leaving unguarded the prize of all these weeks of complex villainy? Stay! More likely this was another of his subtle strategems, a trap baited cunningly to rob us of all caution. What could suit him better than to leave her thus and, doubling back without her knowing of it, to shoot us down from behind the roadside thicket as we sprang from our carriage, reckless with delight?

As if in answer to my thought Mr. Sackville took my second pistol from the cushion where I had laid it, and held it cocked and ready. But as Barry drew our horses to a stand he dropped it with an exclamation of disgust. The slender shape in blue had turned toward us and, framed in Felicity's close bonnet, revealed the face of Hebe.

She stood before us quietly, even submissively, almost too ready to be questioned — I thought — but with more than a suggestion of insolence in the smile that lurked about her beautiful mouth. Mr. Sackville ignored her, however, walked straight to the door of the chaise, pulled it open, peered in and felt about, tossing the traveling rugs this way and that.

"Robert," he said, turning to me, "will you be kind enough to stand at the horses' heads while Barry transfers Miss Felicity's trunk from the rack of the chaise to our carriage?

"And now, my girl," he asked quietly, placing himself in front of Hebe and fixing her with a keen but not unkindly glance, "be so good as to tell me where you have left your master and mistress."

130

"They left me, Mr. Sackville," she replied with the suspicion of a titter in her soft tones. "Just after the chaise broke down a gentleman came along in his coach and four. He was going to New York and had plenty of room. So he took them in."

"Then, if we wish to overtake them, we had better press on at once?" Mr. Sackville asked with a show of eager satisfaction.

"Yes, sir. I should think you had better, as quick as you can," she replied, her small even teeth flashing in a smile. "He said he meant to sweat his horses, that gentleman did."

"Perhaps we cannot hope to catch him in that case." Mr. Sackville looked discouraged. "Perhaps we had better return and leave what we have for Monsieur de Saint Loup at his house in New Dortrecht."

"Oh, no, sir!" The girl bit her lip on the exclamation, but went on quickly. "The gentleman said he meant to stop somewhere. So you could catch up with him then."

"About midnight, should you think?"

"Yes, sir. The gentleman said he aimed to stop about midnight."

"And although he had plenty of room and four horses, he couldn't take you and even Miss Felicity's light trunk because the extra weight would delay his progress, I suppose."

"That was it exactly, sir," the girl agreed, her contempt for his benignant guilelessness plain to be read in her insolent eyes.

"And your mistress left you her warm furred pelisse lest you should become chilled while you kept guard over her luggage, I take it."

"Yes, sir."

Mr. Sackville turned to Barry, who had resumed his place on the box by this time.

"Turn the carriage round, Barry," he directed. "We are going back to New Dortrecht with all speed.

"As for you, wretched woman," he exclaimed sternly, "you will come with us. You will show us precisely where your master caused your mistress to leave this vehicle with him and tell us how he planned to return to his house."

"I will tell you nothing," she flashed at him. "I — I have told you the truth already, sir," she added sullenly.

"No," he replied quietly. "You have told me only the falsehoods your master bade you tell. No coach and four, no vehicle of any kind, has gone by here since your accident. The tracks in the mud show that. As for your mistress's pelisse, which you are wearing, I have seen your own cloak; I remember it. It would have served every purpose, save the one of causing me to hear in every village that a post-chaise had

131

passed through with a lady in a furred blue pelisse at one of the windows. Monsieur de Saint Loup has doubled back with your mistress, from some farmhouse probably, where he could hire a gig. All he had to do was to keep off the road until we had gone by. To Miss Felicity, I suppose, he pretended that, moved by her entreaties, he was taking her back to her home, and that the gig would be quicker than the chaise on these bad roads. Am I right?"

"I told you what did happen," the girl insisted sulkily.

"You stick to that? Very well." The rector spoke with telling gravity. "Since you do, I will take you on to this village and hand you over to the constable as a thief, whom I have caught on the road with her owner's luggage and wearing her mistress's clothes."

"You will do exactly as you like about that, of course," she returned with haughty indifference.

"You have seen the inside of the usual village lock-up?" Mr. Sackville inquired. "You know that all the prisoners are herded together in one small room, any woman at the mercy of the men — unless the jailor should happen to take a fancy to her?"

She sneered at him openly at that:

"You cannot frighten me so. You would never leave me to such a fate — you, a gentleman, a minister of the gospel."

"Sooner than leave your mistress in the hands of that miscreant who calls himself Comte de Saint Loup I will, and I think I am doing God's work by doing so. Come along at once."

His tone was so level, his face so deadly white, and the hand he laid upon her shoulder so strong and steady, that she cowered under it, all her effrontery vanished. She poured forth her confession. Things had gone as he guessed. Saint Loup had taken Felicity from the chaise at a farmhouse on the far side of the last town but one, when he learned that he could hire a gig there. By this time he must be well on his way back to his house by Gallows Hill with her. If he approached it by the back road and kept the curtains drawn, he might count on exercising his villainy undisturbed there for as long as it would have taken Mr. Sackville and me to return from our pursuit of the chaise; and with luck we might have been lured into following that vehicle all the way to New York.

The wretched girl ended in a burst of weeping and a clamorous appeal for protection — all her fine airs of the highly trained courtesan that she was, swept away by terror of Saint Loup's vengeance. He would kill her slowly, she cried, starve his great hound for a week and then toss her, bound, gagged and naked, into the creature's kennel, as he had often promised to do if she betrayed him.

"You need have no further fear of Saint Loup," Mr. Sackville assured her with a grimness that carried conviction even to her terrified mind. "Go on and carry out the rest of his orders, however. Leave his luggage wherever he told you to. Then go to the rector of Trinity Church, if you wish decent employment, and — "

"I — I really don't, sir," she interrupted with something of her usual self-possession. "When I can live like a lady why should I slave as a servant? Madame Georges can always find places for girls like me."

"At least you are honest about it," he said with a wry smile, and tossed away the sheet from his notebook on which he had begun to write.

"Now why," I asked when we had left her and, once more in my uncle's carriage, were lumbering back along the road toward home — "Now why has Saint Loup chosen to double back? Is it that he could not forego the luxury of that bridal chamber which he prepared with such care, or had he forgotten something essential to him in the haste of his departure this morning?"

"I suspect," Mr. Sackville replied gravely, "that he knew of no other place which he could reach so quickly, where he could count on twenty-four hours of the absolute seclusion necessary for the wickedness which he longs to perpetrate."

The thought was plausible enough, and dreadful enough — God knows — to have made me ponder. But my thoughts had run ahead of his speech so that I burst out:

"Suppose that he has discovered the whereabouts of old Peter's secret hoard, that he had neither the time nor the opportunity to remove it to his carriage without the postilion's guessing at its nature! His chaise came down the hill without him, remember. He must have walked. So — "

"Possibly," the rector began. Then, clutching my arm: "Old Peter's ghost! Did it ever walk between the day of Saint Loup's departure for New York to get his things and the arrival of his hound? Nobody could answer that question now, I suppose. But the disappearance of Peter's clothes at the time of his death . . . I kept asking myself who could have taken them. Who but the murderer? But the murderer was a wolf, and a wolf doesn't steal clothes — unless it is a wolf that can resume the shape of a man at will."

He pulled down the glass in the door, leaned out into the rain and called to Barry:

"Stop at the next post-house and get horses. Push these poor beasts as much as they'll stand until then."

It was well for us that the post-house was no farther off
133

than it was. My uncle's horses, excellent though they were, had long passed their prime and, soft from the easy life and light duty which he required of them, drew up with heaving flanks and quivering knees at the end of their journey. Meanwhile, moreover, the weather had begun one of those swift changes so characteristic of that valley, which is an open corridor from north to south. A wind howled down its length, stiffening the ruts of the muddy road and driving the rain before it with ever-increasing volleys of sleet. By the time we set out again behind fresh horses it was skimming the mudholes with ice, into which our wheels plunged crackling. The blowing snow all but hid the roadside walls and fences, and through the gathering of the early darkness the carriage lamps showed no more than a heaving surface of white with, here and there, the furrow left by some more heavily laden vehicle winding through it.

Progress over this congealing quagmire at the speed which Mr. Sackville exhorted Barry to maintain rendered speech, and thought itself, impossible. After we had verified the girl's story at the farmhouse where Saint Loup had obtained the gig we exchanged hardly a word, so occupied were we with the task of keeping from being hurled pell-mell into the bottom of the carriage as it lurched and bounded behind the plunging horses.

Once or twice in some brief stretch of smoother going I drew my breath to ask Mr. Sackville what he meant to do when we reached the town, or I strove to pin my mind to the making of some plan of my own. But before a word could be spoken or two thoughts arranged together, the cushion would fall away beneath me, the arm-sling creak with the weight I threw upon it. Then the rector's great shoulder would drive the wind from beneath my ribs, as my side of the carriage sank swiftly, and we would be thrown helter-skelter into the corner of the seat.

Anxiety lest even that sturdy vehicle should collapse under such punishment, or one of the horses break neck or legs in one of the hidden pitfalls of the road and leave us stranded in that wilderness of mud and snow, was all my mind was entertaining. Even a sense of the passage of time ceased to function. For after what seemed an eternity made up of continual buffetings and bruises I was nevertheless surprised when the carriage stopped and by the light of a great square lantern that swung above the roadway I recognized the familiar outlines of the first houses of New Dortrecht through the swirling snow.

Mr. Sackville had the door open and was out upon the road before I could collect my scattered wits and gather my stiffened legs under me.

134

"Drive to the tavern and remain there with the carriage ready for instant use, Barry," He directed. "It will be soon enough for your master to hear of our return when Mr. Farrier and I have leisure to tell him of it. Follow me, Robert." And without another word he led the way up the steep street towards Gallows Hill at a pace that made me pant to keep up with him.

Dark as it was, I knew that road so well that I could recognize each spot that bore some memory of the monstrous happenings which had followed the advent of the strange and terrible man whom we pursued. There was the alley's end where mad little Aggie had clawed and spat at him and he had cowed her savage cur with a glance and a growling imprecation on the day of his arrival. Here, with murder in my heart, I had lurked for him that very morning, which now seemed so infinitely remote. Here was a place, which for no reason at all recalled my hurrying through the twilight of that first snowstorm to meet Felicity in the shelter of Gallows Hill and learn of her love for me at the cost of the use of my right arm. And finally we halted on the spot where Saint Loup and I had stood on the spot where Saint Loup and I had stood in the warm autumn sunshine and old Peter had cursed him and ordered us away.

All at once I felt in my breast a kind of lightness, such as a traveler feels at the sight of home. Had I traveled a full circle from that day to return and put an end to this chain of horrors at the point where they began? Was I indeed at my journey's end? The house, a mere dark mass against the loom of the pine wood behind it, looked hardly promising for an outcome. Not a crevice of light showed in its low front. If smoke issued from its chimneys it was lost like their tops in the scudding gloom of the night. But I thrust my hand into my pocket and gripped the butt of my pistol as Mr. Sackville tried the gate.

It was locked with a large padlock, and under his impatient hands a heavy chain clanked noisily. Spiked on top, with a four-foot wall and the roadside ditch to flank it, this gate delayed us. But, three or four minutes later, we were stealing round the house toward the back door, when a pale glow of light in front of us brought us to a stand. It slowly advanced, the snowflakes circling and zig-zagging into and out of the arc of its illumination, the line of the shadow of the angle of the house, from behind which it came, sweeping closer and closer across the snow-covered ground to the spot where we crouched together against the foundation wall.

Then, had I not been prepared in every way against such a delusion, I think I should have believed that old Peter's restless spirit stood before me. The old green redingote showed plainly

135

in the lantern-light, and through the lantern's perforated metal top lancets of light shot up to speckle floating locks of gray and half reveal a cadaverous face and cavernous eyes. As it was, my hand faltered on my weapon. Mr. Sackville himself was unmoved.

"Saint Loup, yield yourself. Stand or you die!" he cried out.

The figure did not start. It made no visible movement. Simply the light went out, leaving us blinded by the sudden darkness. I felt rather than saw the rector spring forward, and heard his low cry of satisfaction as his foot struck the lantern lying where it had fallen in the snow. It flickered as he lifted it, and burned up suddenly in a steady flame. Then he had caught me by the arm and was pulling me toward the kitchen door.

"Have your pistols out and cocked," he whispered. "You must stand guard while I force an entrance. De Retz, the wolf, the villain in his proper form, may oppose us next. We fight with Proteus, remember. Ha! Fire! Oh, fire!"

We must still have been a dozen feet from the stone steps which old Peter and the lawyer's clerk had stained with their blood, when in the instant of his warning cry I saw a shadow move upon them as it had moved that night when Killian and I had closed in upon the empty house. My left arm flew up, and I fired at some huge shapelessness that hurtled at me through the air. It dropped a yard from our feet, rolled over with a howl of pain and the gnashing of savage jaws, and was lost where the high curbing of the wellhead made the darkness impenetrable.

Thrusting before him with his long staff, the rector leapt into this obscurity. His great voice rang through the garden till the pine wood flung it back:

"After him! The other pistol — quick!"

I too sprang forward, but it was over his shoulder that I sent the second silver missile whizzing at the vague shape that rose to meet us. It leapt upward and backward to the top of the curbing as I fired, poised there, rampant, while we two recoiled before the miracle. For it was no hairy beast that confronted us, but the fat, naked shape of him who called himself Saint Loup. Within the gallows-like framework of the well he wavered above us for an instant, so close that we could see the oozing wounds which my bullets had torn through his breast, so close that the feral reek of his body on that tingling air made my gorge rise, so close that the glare of his eyes was in our eyes and we heard the grinding of his teeth as his hatred of us fought its short, fierce fight with deadly weakness. Then his knees bent beneath him, the small round belly swung

136

between the sagging thighs, the head snapped back, chin to the sky, and with arms flung wide he dropped backward into the mouth of the well.

XIX. – THE COUNTER-WEIGHT

How long we continued to stand, frozen with horror, after that muffled crash upon the water fifty feet below I cannot tell. Mr. Sackville was the first over its verge, listening, and all but went to his death in doing so. The masonry, old and long neglected, gave beneath his weight, and he barely saved himself as the great stones, bounding from side to side, rushed down to the unseen depths.

"Here! Put your shoulder to it!" he called to me as, released from my stupefaction, I was springing toward the house. "She is safe now. Heave with me here. We'll make assurance doubly sure. The whole wall is rotten."

Entire segments toppled to our thrust, crashed sparkling against the stony sides and boomed as they smote the water. It was the work of three minutes perhaps before all that remained was a lipless orifice beneath the two uprights and the cross-beam with the bucket-chain and counter-weight depending from it. There was no sound of water, only the dry crash of stone on stone, as the last shards of masonry struck bottom. The wreckage had filled the spring-fed cavity to a point above the water level.

How we smashed our way into the house and snatched one glimpse of the dainty supper table in the little salon – the used dishes and empty wine bottles on one side of it, the untouched plate and brimming glass on the other – before we burst the lock of the bedroom door I need not tell. How we found Felicity in the corner farthest from that painted bed, and in what tattered disarray, her wrists pinioned and ankles hastily bound with a silken rope from the curtains, I will not. She flung a gallant smile at us; I ran to her and severed her bonds; Mr. Sackville wrapped her in his cloak; and she went limp and unconscious in his arms.

"Fetch some wine, Robert," he directed, moving to lay her on the bed. "There's a decanter of what looks like Madeira on the sideboard out there. Then run for Barry and the carriage."

I turned toward the door to obey him, and staggered back three steps, I believe, from the sight that met my eyes. Saint Loup stood in the doorway – Saint Loup whose body, pierced by bullets, must lie naked and drowned beneath a ton of shattered masonry at the bottom of the well. Yet there he stood, dressed in his own smallclothes and shoes and stockings, with old Peter's green redingote buttoned up to his chin. His face was livid, his upper lip lifting spasmodically to show the

137

long right canine; but his leaden eyes were steady over the sights of the two double-barrelled pistols with which he covered us, and that deep growling chuckle came from his chest before he spoke. Only his voice, husky and breathless, betrayed the desperate weakness which he was holding at bay.

"Closer — a little closer together, if you please." A movement of the muzzle of the pistol nearest me filled out his words. "I know that you have not thought it necessary to reload, but I cannot risk your rushing me. It would imperil the small chef-d'oeuvre which I have in mind — a work of art, if you will permit me to explain, executed with that economy of means which is the quintessence of artistic creation; no bungling business with two pistols and several hundred-weight of stones in the effort to destroy a single life, but four lives to be taken, each with a single bullet. For I have no intention of lingering on to grace a gallows."

He paused — to master his weakness, I suppose. But I saw his eyelids quiver, and my limbs grew tense for a spring. I was resolved to take his fire in a rush at the last rather than let us be shot down like sheep. Some moments back he had lowered his pistols, only keeping them pointed at us from the height of his waist, and he continued to hold them so, as he began to speak again.

"But as to the details of my composition, Mr. Sackville — that lovely creature in your arms — shall I shoot her as you hold her thre, or will you die first, leaving me to dispose of her as I may think fit?"

For answer Mr. Sackville turned his back upon him, thus making of himself such a bulwark as he could for Felicity's unconscious body.

"Rush him as he fires, Robert," he said quietly.

"Ah, but Robert, mon cher cousin, he is to go first of all," Saint Loup explained suavely. "So only do I see a successful solution of the problem. Before that, however, reverend sir, permit me to talk with you a minute. Permit me to tell you how amazed I am that with your learning and penetration you did not doubt when you seemed to overcome me so easily. The loose stone which I kicked from the inner ledge to make you believe I had fallen to the water below. Until you began pushing the curbing into the well with such enthusiasm I had little hope that you would not suspect my hiding place a small distance down in the side of it. A clutch of the chain, a step or two from one projecting stone to another, and one is perfectly concealed, to be sure. But I had not dared to hope that one of you would not remain on guard while the other entered this house. That clever rector, I said to myself — even the good, stupid Robert — "

He may have ceased just there, or he may have spoken a little further. I do not know. His eyes, save for an occasional side glance to make sure of my quiescence, were fixed on Mr. Sackville who, with his chin upon his shoulder, kept his steady gaze upon his tormentor. But for the past two minutes my faculties had been intent on small sounds that came from some other part of the house. Could it be that anyone else was stirring in that remote neighborhood on such a night, that he had caught some gleam from the shattered door and had moved to investigate? A wild hope leapt within me. The smallest diversion might be enough to enable me to spring upon Saint Loup before he could fire. There was a sound like soft footsteps from the kitchen — but such slow ones, so uncertain. Old Peter himself might have slippered about like that.

And then I all but shouted aloud in my surprise. As I looked past Saint Loup the open door gave me a narrow vista of the little, luxurious salon, a corner of the exquisite table-cloth; the figures in the damask curtains, seen and lost again in the flicker of the fire-light; the shadowy recess of a pier glass above the gilded brackets of a molded console. And into this scene of drowsing ease, the sound of his stocking feet lost in the deep pile of the carpet, his large, white hands gripping that old Ticonderoga musket of his at the "ready," glided my uncle. His face was ghastly beyond even what it had been on the rector's porch that morning, his eyes cavernous within the dark circles that stained his sunken cheeks; but there was no look of conscious elaboration now in the firm lines of mouth and chin; his glance, fixed on the back of Saint Loup's head, never wavered. Just beyond and almost in line with his quarry though I was, I doubt if he was aware of my looking at him or even of my presence.

For my part I strove to wrench my eyes away from him, lest by their intensity they should betray his approach; but I could not, though it seemed to me that my mere consciousness of his proximity screamed out above the suave flow of the Frenchman's taunts. Another instant, though I, and his nearness alone will strike a warning in Saint Loup's brain; but it did not. Fascinated, I watched each foot advance before the other, saw both planted, and caught the unforgotten precision of the well-drilled soldier in the movement that brought the musket to the "present," the forearm horizontal, second finger on the trigger. The muzzle was within two feet of the back of Saint Loup's head, shook there a moment, steadied. . . . And yet that stream of sneering suavity did not cease.

My uncle's locked lips parted, but no sound came from them at once. Then:

"Saint Loup!" he croaked, and instantly cuddled the musket stock against his chin. Saint Loup whirled — I saw his eyes widen — and took the full blast of the musket in his face.

It was late in January before Felicity's shattered nerves were sufficiently recovered for her to leave her room. But a fortnight later, one dry, sparkling day in early February we set out for New York together within the hour after Mr. Sackville had married us in our uncle's drawing-room. The good ship "Dominica," whose master had been a friend of our uncle's school days, only awaited our coming to set sail for Saint Kitts and Port of Spain. Vashti went with us. Our uncle had sent for her as the best possible of nurses the moment he had been made to understand that a prostration of the nerves, rather than any serious physical harm, accounted for Felicity's condition. And under Vashti's vigilant care, strengthened by the magic of sea and sunshine, her thoughts beguiled by romantic landfalls and bright towns shining between the tropic mountains and the surf, she rapidly regained her equanimity and health.

For in the lining of that old green redingote the coroner at Mr. Sackville's suggestion had searched and found old Peter's will. And though it contained not so much as a hint of the hiding place of the miser's hoard, it named me heir to everything of his that could be found. It went to probate; there was not so much as a whisper of contesting it; and I stood to receive that house and ground which, of all places in the created universe, was hateful to me, and the sum of eleven-hundred and thirty-six dollars and eighty-two cents which had been in Squire Killian's hands on the day of old Peter's death. But the sure expectation of such a sum was sufficient for my immediate needs, I thought; and my uncle was so altered by the experiences of that terrible day and night that I had not even to call in Mr. Sackville to persuade him to agree with me. Moreover, now that he had demonstrated his ability to get along without them, his bankers — like all bankers in all times — had become liberal in their offers of credit. So there was no difficulty about his advancing me the money on my note.

Excepting that, old Peter's cunning seemed to have frustrated the fulfillment of his own desires, unless the scrupulous search of the garden, which I planned to make when the snow was gone, should meet with more success than I schooled myself to hope for. There was a rude drawing on the back of the will, a crude outline of the wellhead with the frame, the chain and counter-weight, for raising and lowering the bucket above it. But, jotted down on the margin, in old

Peter's hand, were such brief notes as to the cost and quantities of material as a man makes during a talk with a mason-contractor. So it seemed quite evident that the drawing meant no more than that the old man had been aware of the dangerous condition of his wellhead and had begun to think of repairing it.

Of course, we did not fail to investigate the hiding place in the side of the well, which had so nearly enabled our enemy to destroy us all. In this we had the assistance of the entire coroner's jury within five minutes after they had brought in their verdict of justifiable homicide. The clergy were still regarded as possessing a quasimagisterial power in those days, and the rector's narrative of the events of that dreadful day and night was accepted almost without a question. I was asked to do no more than corroborate his evidence, and my uncle had nothing to tell beyond what he had seen and done after Barry, in direct disobedience of Mr. Sackville's orders, had run to him with the news that we had traced Saint Loup back to the little house on Gallows Hill.

The storm, which might so easily have defeated our efforts, now turned out to have wrought for us. By daylight all trace of Saint Loup's footprints when he had assumed once more the role of Peter's ghost and when, with justice and vengeance crying out upon him in the rector's voice, he had fled back to the porch, was covered by a foot of snow. Its white blanket stretched unbroken to the lip of the black, unguarded orifice of the well. In two places only did we find a sign of that incredible metamorphosis of which one word would have branded our testimony as that of idiots or stupid knaves. In the light snow under the edge of the porch were the impressions of the great pads of the beast as he crouched awaiting our approach; and in the lee of a low fragment of the wellhead, which still stood upright, were one track of wolf and one of man — a naked foot, small, high-arched, as Killian and I had seen it in the ashes of the hearth — to mark the place of that last, involuntary transformation.

Some casual-looking trampling disposed of all these. Nothing else remained to show that we had contended against any but a quite human miscreant or that the wall had not collapsed in the struggle. No questions were asked about the disappearance of De Retz. Somehow an impression got about that the hound had taken his departure with his master in the chaise and had been left in it to continue the journey to New York with Hebe. But indeed Saint Loup's attempted abduction of Felicity had aroused such general indignation that the interest in the precise manner of his death was a good deal obscured by satisfaction at his having met a fate which he

141

so richly deserved.

So it was a very friendly body of jurymen that peered down at Mr. Sackville and me as, one after the other, we lowered ourselves by means of the bucket-chain, passed below a projecting flagstone that concealed some five feet of the wall beneath it from the gaze of anyone looking down from above, and swung off into a narrow cavity which had been excavated in the side of the well. Cut out of the living rock, it represented the work of years by either old Peter or some previous owner of the property. A more perfect hiding place for a miser's hoard I could not imagine. But if it had ever been used for that purpose, it was quite empty now; and one of the jurymen after another emerged from the examination of it, shaking his head with disappointment.

It was late April when we returned. The roads were deep to the point of impassibility. But the ice was long gone from the river, and it was on the deck of the packet-sloop, as we rounded Thunder Mountain and had our first sight of New Dortrecht on our starboard bow, that Felicity gave me the best proof of all of her complete recovery. Her eager hand caught my arm, and she pointed up to where old Peter's roof just showed above the budding trees.

"I want you to take me up there tomorrow morning," she whispered.

"Why?" I asked, looking at her in sudden fear that some morbid fancy might have returned upon her at sight of the place. But she answered me with a confident smile:

"Well, a little bit because I want to prove to myself that I'm not afraid to go, I suppose. I cannot very well go on living here with a potential castle of terrors up there above me. But chiefly I want to find poor old Peter's money for you, and I believe I can."

But I thought she had the former rather than the latter purpose in mind when, early next day, we pushed open the gate into the garden, where the green shoots were beginning to show among the brown stubs of last year's growth. For from that point she made me lead her over every foot of the ground which Mr. Sackville and I had traversed in that last encounter with Saint Loup. My uncle had replaced the wellcurb with a strong paling, and this she gripped firmly with her two small, green-gloved hands while I told her in detail of the last few minutes of that struggle. Insistent though she was, it seemed to me a foolish thing to do. I watched her closely for the first sign of that shadowy look of terror in her eyes, which for so many weeks had lurked there. But I saw instead a more and more brightly kindled interest.

"Robert," she cried out, "the hoard is here, close beside us. It must be. It was hither that old Peter rushed to guard it. Here the wolf killed little Mr. Rogers and flew at you that night when you came up here with Squire Killian. People went where else they would about the premises without its molesting them. At the very last Saint Loup threw himself between you and the well."

"Mr. Sackville and I examined the well carefully, even went down into it," I reminded her. "We felt over every stone in its sides as far down as we could reach."

"But the hiding place need not have been in the well itself. And an old man like Peter would have wished it to be as accessible as possible, for he still had some money to put into it."

"If you mean the curb," I began.

"I don't believe he would have trusted in anything so shaky."

"He had planned to have the curb repaired. You remember the drawing I told you of, on the back of the will."

"I wish you could get that will from the courthouse long enough for me to look at that drawing," said she. But while she spoke her eyes were busy about the well, the weatherworn uprights and cross-beam of the framework, the rusty chain running up to us out of the dark depths, the iron wheel and the concrete block strapped with iron, which formed the counter-weight.

"Robert!" she cried sharply, and shuddered against my side. "Look! Is that one of your silver bullets flattened up there just beneath the iron band?"

I answered indifferently that I didn't believe so. I did not wish to have to go on and give my reasons, which were that I thought it highly unlikely that a silver bullet would have force enough to flatten, especially after passing through Saint Loup's body.

"But it shines like silver," she insisted, tiptoe on the bottom rail of the paling. "Robert, it's a crack, and the shining comes from inside!"

Before she had finished speaking I was on the top rail, holding on by the frame with one hand, in the other the ring and staple from which the weight depended. There was indeed a crack in the concrete, small enough to escape notice no doubt before the winter storms and frost did their most recent work upon it, but now a good quarter inch in width in one place, and backed by something that shone palely in the spring sunshine.

What with the necessity of returning to the town for a rope and a couple of pulleys, a hammer and cold chisel, it was almost noon before I had detached the oblong block and swung it safely over the paling to the tender green of the turf. There a few blows shattered what proved to be hardly more than a shell. The narrowly spaced iron bands had been relied upon to preserve its integrity against any chance encounter with wall or bucket. And we knelt staring at each other across what looked to us like an incalculable heap of gold and silver coins. Stacked in rows, by far the greater part of them, they had been imbedded in the concrete when it was soft, so that the rows almost touched each other. Only at the top a small slit had been left under the iron, by which the last or three additions to the hoard had been slipped in and wadded with sheep's wool, now moldy by age and wet, to keep them from clinking.

It would take several stout sacks and a small cart to move all that dully glittering treasure at once. But neither of us made a move toward going for them. Fortune, the jade! When she does turn her face toward one, she pours her favors into one's lap with such a contemptuous prodigality, one is fairly ashamed to take them. We knelt there a long time without speaking.

Then Felicity gave a slow sigh and stretched her hand across to touch mine.

"I wish you all the happiness in the world in this," said she, but there was little of happiness in her tone.

"And I you," I answered. "It was only for you that I ever wanted it."

"Oh, as for me," she cried, "I have wished to be poor with you to show you how much I love you. I wish it still."

I had to get up and come round and comfort her upon that. And so our uncle and Vashti found us an hour later when, alarmed at our failure to appear at dinner, they came panting up the hill and into the garden.